DEATH THROUGH THE LOOKING GLASS

Also by Richard Forrest

The Wizard of Death

A Child's Garden of Death

Who Killed Mr. Garland's Mistress?
(Mystery Writers of America Edgar Award)

DEATH THROUGH THE LOOKING GLASS

A Novel of Suspense
by Richard Forrest

THE BOBBS-MERRILL COMPANY, INC.
Indianapolis/New York

Published by The Bobbs-Merrill Company, Inc.
Indianapolis New York

Designed by Gail Herzog Conwell
Manufactured in the United States of America

First printing

Library of Congress Cataloging in Publication Data
Forrest, Richard, 1932-
Death through the looking glass.
I. Title.
PZ4.F72887De [PS3556.0739] 813'.5'4 77-15438
ISBN 0-672-52379-5

For

Richard
Christopher
Remley
Katherine
Mongin
Bellamy

1

He awoke with a start.

A stream of early-morning day through the easterly window brushed across his face as he stared up at the unfamiliar ceiling. Alarmed at his momentary disorientation, he sat up abruptly. The other half of the bed was empty. Bea was gone.

The feeling dissipated as he remembered they were spending the weekend at Damon Snow's beach house. He yawned and looked out the window, where a slowly circling sea gull nonchalantly rode the air currents in easy sweeping motions.

The bedroom door cracked back against the wall.

Lyon Wentworth's muscles tensed as he involuntarily shrugged back against the headboard.

"Surprise!"

They tumbled into the room like rampant children and swirled around the bed in a dervishlike dance. Rocco Herbert's six-foot-eight bulk loomed at the foot of the bed as he lifted its legs from the floor and dropped them.

"Wakey, wakey!" the large man's voice boomed.

Robin Thornburton grasped the edge of the sheet as Lyon clutched it to his neck. "Come out of there."

"If that sheet comes down any further, we'll have a second surprise party," Bea Wentworth said.

"What's going on?"

Bea leaned over to kiss him. "Happy birthday, darling."

A beach robe hurtled across the room and entwined itself around Lyon's head and shoulders. "You've got three minutes to get downstairs," Damon Snow said.

They trooped from the room, laughing. Robin turned at the door and gave him a long look. "Hurry up, now."

He leaned contentedly against the pillow and let the luxury of early-morning sluggishness engulf him for a few moments before he jackknifed to the floor and reached for his clothes. He pulled on a rumpled pair of khaki slacks and a tee shirt and stepped into scuffed boat shoes.

In the cramped bathroom Lyon brushed his teeth and made a few comb passes over a shock of sandy-brown hair. He paused as his eyes caught themselves in the mirror. They had a mildly troubled look, which deepened as he frowned at himself. After thirty, birthdays seemed to arrive with alarming frequency, and he wasn't quite sure he was ready for another one. He refused to accept the possibility that today's artificial demarcation might mean life's midpoint. He felt twenty—he gave a short laugh and amended that to twenty-five—and decided to live to ninety so that today would not be a halfway point.

He and Bea had occupied a rear bedroom, so he took the narrow back staircase down to the kitchen. The room was empty, although the stove and counter space were cluttered with used pans and dishes. A piercing laugh, followed by raised voices, echoed through the house from the area of the dining room, and he walked in that direction through the pantry.

Built near the turn of the century for some now-forgotten Hartford scion and his family, the massive frame house was perched at the end of a point overlooking Long Island Sound. The carpenters had obviously served their apprenticeship in nearby ship-building yards, to judge from their use of heavy timbers. The construction had stood the house well, and it was one of the few in the area to survive the ravages of the 1938 hurricane.

Lyon entered the dining room to find the others standing behind their chairs as if awaiting the signal for a formal seating.

"Everyone's here," Rocco said, while eyeing the dishes strewn across the table.

"Where's Giles?" Bea asked.

"Never showed."

Damon Snow raised a glass of champagne. "To Lyon. May he have many more years, with a new book in each one."

"Hear, hear!" Martha Herbert clinked the edge of her glass with a spoon.

At the head of the table was a large crumb cake with one lone flickering candle. "Blow it out," Bea ordered.

Lyon bent over the candle, coughed, and finally managed to expel a breath that extinguished the flame. A glass of champagne was thrust into his hand. "What time is it?"

"Six."

"In the morning?" He looked down at the sparkling wine. "Oh, what the hell." He drained the glass as the others applauded and took seats. The wine caused a small glow in his stomach that gradually reached toward the rest of his body with slim tentacles of warmth.

Eggs Benedict appeared from under chafing dishes as Lyon sliced off thick slabs of crumb cake and Damon poured more wine. Everyone ate ravenously, and Lyon suspected they had been up long before him.

Tapping his glass for silence, Damon stood at the foot of the table. "And who will do first honors?"

"I will." Robin went over to a lowboy and pulled a long, thin package from its place behind it. She marched solemnly toward Lyon, handed him the package, and stood by his side awaiting his response.

As he accepted the package, he looked up into Robin's smiling face. She shifted her weight slightly, and with arms akimbo and hands along the bottom edge of her black bikini, she allowed her elbow to brush lightly against Lyon's shoulder.

Robin was the exuberant eighteen-year-old daughter of Lyon's illustrator, Stacey Thornburton. While chasing over the hills of North Carolina after some beast or other, Stacey had managed to fall from his jeep and fracture his leg in two places, and Robin had been dispatched north with the latest batch of preliminary sketches for Lyon's next children's book.

The proximity of the young girl's bronzed body made Lyon regret that he and Bea hadn't locked the bedroom door and been late for breakfast. The thought was shattered when a sneakered foot careened off his ankle.

"Open the package, dear," Bea said.

The gift wrap fell away to reveal a charcoal portrait. "Hey, that's marvelous. The way I'd like to look, or maybe the way I looked ten years ago." He half-stood to give Robin a buss and felt her lips linger on his a brief moment.

"NEXT!" Bea yelled and leaned over to whisper in Lyon's ear, "For a moment, I thought you were going to have her for dessert."

Rocco Herbert handed him a package. "To help on the next case."

"THERE WON'T BE A NEXT CASE!" Bea said as Lyon unwrapped a book containing the complete works of Dashiell Hammett.

"Thanks, Chief. Next time we'll both be as hard-boiled as Sam Spade, right?"

"WRONG!" Bea said.

"And now for the *pièce de résistance*." Damon stepped through the door and returned in a moment carrying a bulky package as tall as himself. "Actually it's not just from me," he said as Lyon began to remove the wrapping surrounding the oversized gift, "but from everyone at Cedarcrest Toys."

"My God!" Lyon said as the last of the tissue fell away to reveal a six-foot Wobbly doll. The benign monster, a creation from his first children's book, stared out over the group with a ferocious but essentially kind visage.

Robin clapped. "That's fantastic."

"Isn't it," Bea said with a half-smile at the young girl.

"The first of its kind," Damon said. "A couple of department store buyers saw it in my office the other day and are fighting to have orders filled." He poured more wine. "This time a toast to Robin's father, designer of the first Wobbly." He raised his glass. "And at the risk of sounding mercenary—the most successful item I have in all our lines, although most aren't as big as this fellow."

Lyon looked over the rim of his glass toward Damon Snow at the foot of the table. The toy manufacturer and their weekend host was tall and thin to the point of gauntness. The deeply etched features on the elongated face often made Lyon think of Ichabod Crane.

As Lyon admired Kimberly Ward's gift of a bottle of Dry Sack sherry, Bea left the room and returned with a live white duck in her arms. As she thrust it toward

 Lyon, the outraged bird voiced its indignation.

"If this is lunch, count me out."

"Darling, you've forgotten the Montgolfiers."

"The French balloonists?"

"Uh huh. And what did they send up in their first hot-air-balloon flight?"

A broad smile creased Lyon's face. "A duck and a chicken."

"Let's look outside."

The empty hot-air-balloon bag of the Wobbly II lay properly stretched out along the ground. A wicker gondola, with teakwood control panel and leather along its base, stood upright at the end of the balloon envelope.

Lyon stared awestruck at the new basket. "My God, it's beautiful! Where did you get it?"

"I had it made. BALLOON GONDOLAS ARE NOT EXACTLY SOLD IN THE SUPERMARKET!"

Bea needed a new battery for her hearing aid, but he decided not to comment. "We'll have to try it out."

"I thought you would, but first look at this." She ran her fingers along the small control panel.

"A built-in propane lever."

"No more cricks in the neck from having to use the lever over your head."

He shook his head. "I always thought you hated my balloon."

"I do, but as long as you persist in your madness, you may as well go in style."

He turned to the others, who stood smiling in the background. "I'm going up; let's inflate."

Out of long-practiced habit, Bea and Kim began to spread the balloon envelope as Lyon started the portable air compressor and directed its flow into the bag.

"I need a turkey."

Kim and Bea shook their heads simultaneously and continued studiously to unfold the envelope.

"I'll be chaser," Rocco offered.

"I'll help if you'll tell me what the turkey does," Damon said.

Lyon spread the balloon bag's opening and beckoned to Damon. "You go inside and extend your arms as wide as you can. That helps the thing fill faster."

Damon shrugged and stepped inside the balloon. "I've never even seen one of these things before."

"Ah, I'd suggest you step back a little further."

"He's obviously never seen one, or he wouldn't volunteer to be the turkey," Rocco said.

"What's that?" Damon asked from inside the balloon.

"Never mind."

Compressor air began to riffle the sides of the balloon and fill it out. Lyon picked up the heavy propane burner, adjusted the feed and lit the pilot light. He held the burner across his body, braced his feet, and pointed the nozzle through the balloon opening.

"Hold it wide, Damon," he said and pulled the propane-release lever. As the burner lit with a roar, a jagged three-foot flame jutted into the balloon.

"My God! You've singed my eyebrows."

"Get back a little further and hold it wide." Lyon pulled the lever again for a three-second whoosh of flame.

"I was his turkey once," Rocco said. "Never again."

"Do you have to do it this way?" they heard Damon yell over the burner's roar.

"No, but it's faster."

The burner's intense flame heated the air inside the balloon, which quickly began to fill and take shape. In minutes the fifty-foot-long envelope rounded into circular form and rose upright. Lyon attached the guy wires sewn into the balloon's surface to their brackets on the basket, then mounted the propane burner on its gondola brace, immediately beneath the balloon opening. At periodic intervals he gave short bursts of propane, until warm air had filled the balloon to its full size.

The inflated balloon revealed the large Wobbly face painted on its surface. The twenty-five-foot-high monster grinned out over the group.

"How did you get it from our barn?" Lyon asked as he made final adjustments to the basket attachments.

"Rocco brought it down last night."

As the basket began to bob from the ground, Lyon climbed aboard. "There's room for two. Anyone for a ride?"

They looked at him in sober speculation.

"You're not conning me again," Damon said.

"Why does that sign on the side say 'experimental'?" Robin asked.

"The Federal Aviation people require it. It's not a certified aircraft."

Robin's eyes slowly traveled the length of the large sphere dominating the yard. "I think I'll go for a swim," she said and ran toward the beach.

"No takers?" Heads shook as they declined. "Then I hope you'll excuse me for a while."

"Can we stop you?" Bea asked.

Lyon began his preflight checks and, as always, marveled at the simplicity of the device. He pulled on the lines that were sewn into the nylon envelope, coverging down toward the balloon's opening or appendix. He checked the appendix, where the lines were attached to the load ring, which supported the basket and the propane burner immediately over his head. His periodic firing of the burner would heat the air within the envelope and cause the vehicle to become buoyant. The craft's rate of ascent or descent would be controlled by the amount of propane burned and by the release of hot air from the bag through the panel, a portion of the envelope that opened and closed at his tug on a line. For an emergency descent, Lyon could pull the red cord of the ripping panel, a portion of the bag that, torn away, would spill large amounts of hot air into the atmosphere.

The gondola held a large propane tank and a few instruments: propane gauge, temperature gauge, compass, altimeter, and a variometer. The final piece of equipment was a CB radio.

Lyon pulled the lever for a five-second burn and felt the basket lift from the ground. All was in order, so he signaled to Bea to cast off the mooring line.

After another short burn the balloon began a rapid and noiseless ascent. The clear morning was nearly windless, and the progress was straight up, with little drift. At chimney height Lyon looked down at the dispersing group on the ground. Damon was walking slowly toward the boat house, Bea has gone into the main house, while Robin was a flash of arms twenty yards offshore. Kim had spread a blanket on the sand and lay face down in the warmth.

"You'll never get sunburned this time of the morning," Lyon heard Rocco yell at the basking Kim.

"I don't burn," the black woman retorted with a snort. Kim had been Bea Wentworth's administrative assistant for several years when she was in the state Senate, and now, after his wife's election to the office of secretary of the state, Kim had been appointed deputy secretary. Kim had accepted the appointment with protest, bemoaning the fact that somehow it wasn't quite in keeping with her activist positions to handle corporate registrations for the state of Connecticut.

Rocco walked toward the pickup truck which would act as balloon chase vehicle. He squeezed his two-hundred-eighty-pound frame into the driver's seat and, from years of habit as Murphysville's chief of police, flipped on the truck's CB radio.

The balloon rose silently as it separated itself from the world below. Spotting clouds at fifteen hundred feet that were scudding in an easterly direction toward the water, Lyon leveled at six hundred feet by minute burns of propane. He found himself drifting slightly toward the west along the coastline, at a speed of four knots.

He felt a nostalgic twinge as he passed over the beach house. They had surprised him with a ceremony for a day he had intended to let pass without ceremony. They were the ones he felt closest to: his wife; Rocco, his oldest friend, who had served with him in Korea; Damon Snow, a business acquaintance at first, now becoming a friend; and Robin. The Wentworths had welcomed Lyon's illustrator's daughter when she had arrived for her visit, as if she were a partial and temporary replacement for the daughter they had lost so long ago.

His thoughts of Robin were unsettling. He had the vague fear that her lingering looks and mild flirtations had taken on a different character than that of surrogate daughter. He smiled; the thoughts of the long-limbed young girl were a sure sign of his approaching middle age.

Lyon leaned on the edge of the gondola to watch the slowly passing panorama. Over the water, to the east, the sun balanced on the horizon and cast red streaks across the sound. Looking due south he could see Orient Point, Long Island; below him were passing the cottages along the shore of Lantern City.

He flipped on the CB radio. "Rocco, I can bring her down at the Lantern City football field in half an hour."

"I'll be there."

"Thank you." He flipped off the radio and placed it

back on its mountings and let himself become immersed in the feeling of freedom as he merged with the sky.

The distant pitched whine of a low-flying aircraft destroyed the mood, and he turned to glare toward the offending buzz as occupants of a sailboat might at a power launch. The plane approached from the east, directly out of the sun, and he could catch only fleeting glimpses of it as it banked.

There was only one person in the state who flew such a garishly painted Piper. Tom Giles, long-ago classmate and Hartford attorney, had often passed the Wobbly II in his early-morning flights. Occasionally, when they came across each other at parties given by mutual friends, they would argue the respective merits of their craft.

Tom had come to the party after all. As Lyon watched, the small plane changed to a southeasterly heading. He thought it amusing that Tom still found it necessary to satisfy some inner need by flamboyant displays of his flying, as if adult life had never been quite fulfilling, never so successful as the triumphs of his younger years.

Those early weeks at Greenfield Preparatory had been painful for Lyon. The first day had begun badly. Warned by an alumnus that white bucks were "in," Lyon had arrived for the first day's classes wearing a pair of his father's white medical shoes. The situation had deteriorated from there, and he quickly discovered that his status as a "Townie" was somewhere between a Typhoid Mary and a Russian spy, and on some days he wasn't quite sure of the exact order.

They caught him in the third week. He had rounded a corner in the locker room and inadvertently stumbled on several of his classmates smoking. In his naïveté he had undoubtedly looked shocked at this abuse of the rules. Four of them had jumped him.

"They've gone," were the first words Tom Giles had spoken to him. "Get up off the floor."

Lyon looked up, brushed away the residue of a bloody nose, and saw Tom sitting on the radiator, with one knee pulled up under his chin. "I'll cream them," Lyon had mumbled in youthful bravado.

"You and what army? Come on, man, you've got to get with it. Townies have a choice. You can run home from class every day, become the class clown, or be a jock."

"I'm lousy at basketball."

"Football?" Tom looked reflectively at Lyon as he got to his feet. He appraised Lyon's recently acquired six feet of height and his slight build. "Forget football. How about baseball?"

"Never played."

"Oh, Jesus. Come on, Went. You've got to do something. Everybody does something."

"I have a great butterfly collection."

Giles closed his eyes. "Sorry I asked. You mention butterflies to anybody else at Greenfield and they'll break your back and flush you."

"I've never been great at sports. We traveled a lot, and my skills are . . ."

Giles snapped his fingers. "Lacrosse. We've got a great lacrosse team at Greenfield."

"I've never even seen it played."

"That's the great part. No one else has either, until they come here. You ever seen guys playing sandlot lacrosse, playing lacrosse in their backyards?"

"Well, no." Lyon thought a moment. "Then everybody starts off even. Who do I see about it?"

"Me. I'm JV captain."

Lyon's memories of the beginnings of their relationship immediately faded when he saw a plume of black smoke curling back from the front of Tom's craft. He tensed. His hands gripped the edge of the basket as he fixed his attention on the plane's plight. The smoke continued to roll as the plane went into a dive.

As the aircraft neared the water, its angle of descent seemed to increase, and yet it flew under control as the power dive continued. Why didn't Tom pull the nose up, cut the power—any number of things that might save him from destruction?

He would hit the water in moments.

The balloon was directly over the restaurant near the town pier. Lyon glanced quickly at his compass and reached for the CB radio. He switched to channel 9, the emergency channel.

"This is an emergency from Wobbly Two over Lantern City. There is a light plane in distress. Does anyone read me?" He flipped to receive.

"I read you, Wobbly Two. This is Red Ball on the Conn Pike. I am proceeding south. What do you need?"

Lyon switched to transmit. "Thank you, Red Ball. Get word to the Coast Guard." As he watched, the plane hit the water and immediately disappeared. "Get word to the Coast Guard that a small aircraft has gone down in the sound. A heading of 170 from the restaurant at the Lantern City town pier."

"I got you; 170 from the pier. I'm near the State Police barracks, and I'll have them talk to you. Out."

Lyon switched the radio over to channel 24, where Rocco would be monitoring. "Rocco. Rocco. Do you hear me? Do you read me?"

"I'm talking, mister," a high-pitched and astringent voice said in anger.

"This is an emergency."

"Use the emergency channel."

"I'm in the pickup going toward the football field." Rocco's voice overrode the woman's.

Lyon looked down from the balloon. "I'm over the Lantern City town beach. Get over here fast."

"I can see you. Be right there."

Lyon flipped back to the emergency channel with one hand while the other pulled the red rope of the ripping panel. "Sergeant Raskin here. Who wants the Coast Guard?"

"A plane has gone down at a bearing of 170 from the town pier. I estimate about six thousand yards out."

The open panel spilled gusts of hot air from the envelope of the balloon, and Lyon had to replace the radio and attend to the rapid descent of the balloon. He flipped the propane burner for very short burns and looked down at the onrushing beach.

The balloon's rate of descent was alarming, and he could only hope he would hit the slim sandy beach rather than the water, that he would not fall onto some of the large rocks spotted along the shore.

Rocco pulled the pickup truck into the adjacent parking lot as the balloon landed with a heavy bounce on the beach.

Lyon was thrown against the side of the basket, then flipped over the edge to land unharmed in the sand. He rolled over and onto his feet and ran at full speed toward the truck. Rocco had the door open and the pickup rolling as Lyon threw himself into the cab and gasped for breath.

"Where to?"

"Back to Snow's house. He's got a speedboat tied to his dock. Hurry, Rocco. Tom Giles just went down in the drink."

2

Damon Snow stood at the helm of the motorboat as it bucked through the water at full throttle. As it pulled past the town pier, Lyon tapped him on the shoulder and pointed to the right.

"Straight out from here!" he yelled over the roar of the engines.

The boat swerved in a tight arc toward a new heading that took it directly away from the pier. The violent turn threw Lyon back against the seat as Rocco, standing next to Damon, gripped the windshield with both hands.

"How far out?" Damon yelled.

"Cut your speed at three thousand yards. We don't want to cut him in half if he's in the water."

The bow rose and tide swells slapped the hull as the boat swept straight away from the dock. "Are you sure of your bearing?"

"The bearing, yes, but it's hard to estimate distance over water. He went down directly in front of me when I was over the pier. But the sun was in my eyes."

The engine whine and hull slap decreased markedly as Damon pushed the twin throttles to a one-third-ahead position. Rocco indicated by hand signals that Lyon should search on the port side, he on the starboard, while Damon's position at the wheel would allow him to scan ahead. They were silent as they peered across the water, searching for a swimmer, an oil slick, or any sign of wreckage that would mark the small plane's grave.

After some minutes Damon turned to Lyon: "We're pretty far out. Suppose I go to port a hundred yards and sweep back toward shore?"

"Fine," Lyon replied and pointed. "We're going to have help. That looks like a Coast Guard cutter."

The cutter pulled alongside the motorboat, and while her commanding officer and Lyon held a shouted interchange, the two boats were joined by a Lantern City police launch. The cutter dropped a red marker buoy at the spot Lyon felt was the closest to the plane's crash point. They divided the area into grids and began a series of careful search patterns.

After two hours of fruitless search, a police officer in the launch signaled for Damon to head back to his dock. They turned back, followed by the police boat, as the cutter continued its methodical search.

As soon as they reached the dock, and before Damon had an opportunity to secure the mooring lines, Rocco stepped to the pier and strode toward the house. After the boat was docked, Lyon found him in the living room, hunched over the phone.

"This is Chief Herbert. Let me speak to the airport manager. . . . That you, Gary? Rocco Herbert here. No, I don't want a flying lesson. I need information. You know Tom Giles's plane? . . . A Piper with a crazy paint job. . . ." Rocco looked toward Lyon, who nodded affirmatively. "Who took it up? . . . Giles called you yesterday and told you to have it gassed and ready for takeoff. . . . Did it have a radio? . . . We think it might have gone down off Lantern City." He slowly hung up and turned to Lyon.

"Well?"

"No radio. He always flew visual flight rules. It took off yesterday afternoon."

"Yesterday afternoon?"

They both turned as a police officer standing by the doorway cleared his throat. Lyon recognized Lantern City's police chief, Will Barnes. He was a near replica of Rocco, although in a smaller version: a big man with massive shoulders and closely cropped hair.

"You still don't wear a gun," Rocco said. "Or does your mother make you leave it at home?"

"At least I'm not a cat freak, like certain cops I could name."

"Did you find the plane?" Lyon asked impatiently.

"Nope. You Lyon Wentworth?"

"Yes."

"We've put divers down near the buoy marker. Are you sure it went down there?"

"Not positive, Chief. But it's the best estimate I could give the Coast Guard."

Barnes sat in a straight chair and took a small pad from his breast pocket. "I'd like to get a statement from you, Mr. Wentworth. Give me as many details as you can."

"Yes, of course. This morning, in fact early this morning, my wife and friends inflated my balloon, and I took it aloft."

"At what time?"

"I can't give you the exact time. I don't wear a watch."

"About 6:45," Rocco said. "He called me on the radio immediately afterward."

"And what time would you say the plane went down?"

"About seven," Rocco said.

"I also believe the plane was owned by Thomas Giles, a Hartford attorney."

"That seems to check out with the Murphysville airport," Rocco added.

"Are you sure of the sighting you gave the Coast Guard?"

"I don't quite follow the question, Chief Barnes."

Will Barnes closed his notebook and carefully replaced it in his breast pocket. "I don't know how to put this diplomatically, Mr. Wentworth, except to say that we can't find any airplane."

"I've heard of planes going down without a slick or any wreckage floating to the surface."

"Yes, so have I, but not usually in Long Island Sound, a couple of miles offshore. However, we'll continue, and the Coast Guard has a specially equipped cutter in New Haven that they'll have up here tomorrow morning. It carries various sensing devices that will determine whether or not a plane is down."

"'Whether or not?' I saw an airplane go down!"

"So far, we haven't been able to locate anyone else who did."

"It was early." Lyon realized that Will Barnes was trying to be as polite as the circumstances allowed, but he couldn't stop the foam of anger that rose within him. "Officer, I saw an airplane in difficulty, with what appeared to be smoke issuing from the engine cowling, and the airplane went into a power dive that took it into the water."

"Of course. And we will keep searching, Mr. Wentworth. By the way, I assume that is your balloon on the town beach?"

"It is."

"We'd be appreciative if you'd move it as quickly as

possible. It's going to play havoc with the sunbathers."
Will Barnes stood up and walked to the door, then turned to face Lyon. "Had you been drinking this morning, Mr. Wentworth?"

"We had a little for breakfast," Lyon replied as Rocco put a hand to his face.

"For breakfast," Barnes said reflectively. "Tell me, Rocco, is there a charge for operating a hot-air balloon while under the influence?"

Rocco shook his head. "There ought to be."

"YOU COULD BE MISTAKEN!" Bea said as she drove the pickup toward the town beach.

"Your battery's low again."

"What?"

Lyon plucked the minute hearing aid from his wife's ear, banged it twice against the dashboard, then replaced it. "How's that?"

"I said, you could have been mistaken in what you saw."

"The sun was in my eyes, and the visibility and lines of sight were not good—I'll grant that. But I've been up hundreds of times over the years, Beatrice."

"Usually on my days off."

He shook his head. "Be serious. Hundreds of times, and in my whole ballooning career I have seen only one multicolored single-engine airplane like that, and that was Tom Giles's. That's why I continued watching it."

"Then it's down there in the water somewhere."

"It's got to be."

"Then they'll find it, won't they?"

"Eventually."

They drove silently for a few moments before Bea turned to him with a look of mild puzzlement. "By the way, when is Robin going back down south?"

"I don't know. She hasn't said."

"She came up to deliver the drawings and has turned into a permanent house guest."

"I guess it's just a change for her."

"I don't like the way she looks at you."

"Come on, Bea. She's only eighteen."

"That's the second thing."

"You aren't serious?"

"Yep." She turned the truck into the town beach parking lot. They walked over to where Lyon had so hurriedly left the balloon earlier in the day.

He stood over the tilted gondola and looked disconsolately down at the destruction. The altimeter had been torn from the wood paneling, the CB radio and compass were missing, and a long gash had been rent in the balloon envelope, as if someone had maliciously ripped the fabric with a jackknife.

"Sometimes it hardly pays to be a good Samaritan," Bea said as she put a hand on his arm. "I'm sorry, Lyon."

He sat on the end of the dock and let his feet dangle over the water. The sun waned to a red glow in the western sky. Out on the water the Coast Guard cutter had begun to move slowly down the sound, while the police launch retrieved the last scuba diver.

Tom Giles had disappeared into the darkening waters out there. The last cry of Lyon's childhood now whimpered into the black waters of the sound. So many others were gone, or he'd lost track of them; Giles's death would mark the end of a remembered time that would now fade into vague shadows. Their interests had diverged over the years, and often long spans of time had passed without their seeing each other, but at every reunion Lyon had always felt warmth for the long-ago boy who had offered friendship to a gangling adolescent. He sighed. Greenfield would have been years of living hell without Tom's friendship. Again he felt the hovering specter of age.

He heard someone behind him and then felt hands on his shoulders.

"It's turned out to be a lousy day for you."

He looked up at Robin. "I guess I've had better. It had a great start."

"Can I sit with you?"

"Do you always wear that?"

"What?"

"The bathing suit."

She laughed. "In the summertime. It's almost like not having anything on."

Lyon agreed and pointedly looked toward the police boat as it turned in the direction of the dock. "Won't your father be wondering about you?"

"Oh, no. I called last night, and he said for me to stay as long as I'm welcome. I hope I still am."

"Of course you are, Robin. We love having you with us."

She sat next to him and let her legs dangle over the edge of the dock. He felt the pressure of her hip against his, turned that over in his mind a moment, and decided it was accidental. The gentle bumping of her toes against his was not accidental. He inched to the side. The depression that had surrounded him as he moped alone at the dock had disappeared, to be replaced by feelings he preferred not to deal with. The situation had become ludicrous. He was years older than this near child.

He evoked an image of Bea at the house, standing on the long front porch, looking toward the water and dock, her eyes filled with hurt. He realized that he was trying to conjure up guilt for things not done, in order to cope with a nebulous situation. He laughed.

She cocked her head toward him. "What's so funny?"

"Nothing, really. I was thinking about how I almost made a fool of myself."

"Over the airplane?"

"That's as good a thing as any."

"I think you're a wonderful person, Lyon. In fact, I think you're one of the most marvelous men I've ever met."

"I don't often kick sleeping dogs."

"I'm serious. It shows in your books. Take *The Wobblies' Revenge.* It's more than a children's story. It's an allegory for the whole human condition."

"Don't try to read too much into them, Robin. They're entertainment for children."

"You're belittling yourself again. You're always doing that. You shouldn't do it, and she shouldn't do it, either."

"She?"

"Beatrice."

He thought of Bea, their years of marriage, the tragedies and triumphs, the accomplishments . . . how she had supported him while he was finishing college. Then he had gone on to teaching and, later, the first children's book; only then had she begun her own career—first her election to the State House of Representatives, then to the Senate, and last year to secretary of the state. He loved her and knew that she loved him.

"I love you, Lyon."

"I love you, too."

"I knew you did."

"My God, Robin! I was thinking of someone else!" He saw the pain cloud her eyes. "I mean, it's not the same. Bea and I both care for you. We consider you almost as a replacement for the daughter we lost."

"That wasn't how I meant it."

"You need someone your own age. Someone with talent, a zest for life that will allow both of you to . . ."

"You have what I want."

At full throttle the police boat turned toward the dock, throwing a sheet of foamy spray to each side of the prow. Chief Barnes stood in the cockpit and waved to Lyon. "I think we have company," Lyon observed.

As the launch cut speed and pulled to the side of the dock, Lyon grasped the mooring line and cleated it around a stanchion. Will Barnes jumped to the dock from the still-rocking boat. "We can't find it, Wentworth."

"I'm sure it's out there."

"I know you are," the police officer said, with a dubious quality to his voice. "But I've been out there all day, and the only thing I've gotten is a hell of a sunburn."

"Damn it all, Barnes, I know what I saw!"

"Yeah, well . . . we've got to give it up for now. If it's out there, eventually something will surface." He stepped back into the boat as Lyon cast off the line. The launch reversed engines, slid back from the dock, and made a tight turn toward the town dock.

"We had better go back to the house," Lyon said.

Robin stared at him for a long moment; then her shoulders gave an almost imperceptible shrug. As he turned, her hand slid into his, and they walked back to the house, where Bea sat in a rocker on the porch, looking toward them with opaque eyes.

The day's events cast a pall over the dinner table that even Damon's sly witticisms over Lyon's ballooning failed to break. By mid-evening, excuses were being made and subdued farewells spoken, and the house party broke up.

Robin volunteered to drive the pickup carrying the balloon, while Bea drove Lyon in the Datsun. He looked at her out of the corner of his eye as she drove toward

 Murphysville with a concentrated effort, her lips pursed. "I accidentally said a silly thing today."

She didn't answer for a count of four. "Do I have a choice from column A or column B?"

"It was to Robin."

"That's column A."

"She told me how much she liked us, and I replied that we liked her also."

"Is that the editorial or the regal we?"

"Me."

"I wonder if we could put her in a cage and mail her back down south."

"You don't mean that?"

"DAMN IT ALL, LYON! A couple of more birthdays and you'll qualify as a dirty old man. Right now, I think you're in that confused in-between state."

The pickup passed them doing seventy. Its horn honked, and they saw Robin waving until she sped around a distant curve.

It was nearly ten when they pulled into the drive at Nutmeg Hill. Robin had arrived before them and was already in bed. Bea yawned, looked at him inquiringly, and then went silently upstairs.

Unable to sleep, he debated having a glass of sherry or attempting to get some work done on the new book. He went into the study to sit at the desk that overlooked the river below the promontory. His partially completed *Danny Dolphin* lay at the right of the typewriter, and he absently riffled through the yellow pages.

Any creativity concerning the playful but wise dolphin seemed far removed from his present state of mind. He poured a pony of sherry. When the phone rang he frowned and reached for the receiver. He knew the content of the call. It would be either Rocco or Chief Barnes confirming Giles's death. He mumbled an acknowledgment into the phone.

"What's the matter, Went? You squiffed?"

Lyon's hand shook and he had to clench the phone to still the tremors. "Giles? Tom Giles? Is that you?"

"Hell, what did we used to say? No, it's Yehudi. Of course it's me."

"I saw your plane go down. Your Piper with the crazy color scheme. I saw it go down in the sound earlier today."

"Right now, Went, the damn plane is the least of my worries. If it's gone, I get the insurance money. Got a problem just a little more important." The voice on the other end of the line tried to laugh, but the result was hollow and tinged with fear. When Tom continued, his tone was somber and distant. "I'm in trouble, Went. I need help, and I need it desperately."

"What is it?" Lyon fought to sort out his confusion.

"I have good reason to believe someone is trying to kill me."

"Come over to the house—now."

"No. I need someone here. A witness I can trust. Will you come?"

"Of course. Your house?"

"No, I'm at the lake cottage. Make it fast, Went. Like the old cross shot . . . faster than that."

"I'll get Rocco Herbert to come with me."

"Jesus, not the police! At least not yet. The cottage on Crystal Lake, Went. North side, sixth from the junction. I need to talk with you alone first."

The receiver went dead, and Lyon slowly replaced it on the cradle. He felt tired and bewildered. An airplane had crashed and couldn't be found; its owner called at midnight and said he was going to be killed. . . . The day wasn't the shambles he had thought; it had turned into an inscrutable puzzle.

3

In order to not disturb Bea, he slipped quietly from the house. He released the emergency brake of the Datsun and let the small car roll partly down the drive before turning the ignition key and switching on the lights. At the highway he turned east, toward the outskirts of town.

At one time the hills surrounding Crystal Lake had been forested, and logs had been rolled into the lake to be floated to a sawmill. After cutting the desirable timber, the company had sold off the building lots in a haphazard manner. Second-growth timber now bracketed a hodgepodge of contemporary split-levels near the head of the lake and fishermen's shacks and summer cottages along the far sides.

Lyon turned off at the north junction and began to count to the sixth house. He pulled into a narrow, rutted drive between two pines and parked. The small house, nestled at the edge of the lake, was dark and desolate-looking. He stepped from the car and called out, "Tom! Tom Giles. You here?"

His voice faded into the pines. The front door was locked; as he walked along the side of the house, he found steps that entered onto a redwood deck that protruded out over the water. The double glass door leading off the deck was also locked.

The discovery of a securely locked house as the final event of the last eighteen hours made him consider the possibility that he was the victim of a massive practical joke. The probability that Tom Giles would go to this extreme seemed remote, just as the near-hysterical phone call seemed out of character for the boisterous attorney. He began to try windows along the edge of the house, and on the third attempt he found one unlatched. He slid it open on its aluminum runners and stepped over the sill.

He felt along the wall of the darkened interior until his hand passed over a switch that turned on two table lamps. He was in a long and comfortable room that ran the length of the house and was oriented toward the side of the building that fronted on the water. The furniture was old but serviceable. Built-in bookcases lined the far wall, and a cursory glance informed him that most of the volumes concerned colonial and Revolutionary War history.

Another wall was lined with photographs arranged in chronological order, the later ones showing Giles beside the multicolored plane. Then there were a few conspicuously blank places on the wall. Lyon imagined the missing pictures were from Tom's Washington years and had probably consisted of signed photographs of Nixon and Mitchell. Toward the end were the pictures from his Greenfield days, including the photograph of their senior lacrosse team—Tom in the center as captain and Lyon relegated to the rear of the group, which was reserved for the subs. Lyon paused beside the last photograph. It showed the steps of the Greenfield Library in their last year of school. Lyon's butterfly collection, neatly mounted in cases, was aligned along the library steps. Lyon and Tom, arm in arm, were smiling in the foreground.

In the far corner, next to the telephone table, a chair had been overturned next to a reddish-brown spot on the floor.

The beds in the two empty bedrooms were neatly made. He picked up the phone to call Rocco and found the line dead. It took only minutes to discover the severed phone line dangling from an outside corner of the house.

Martha Herbert held a novel across the front of her long housecoat and squinted up at Lyon from under a mass of oversize plastic hair curlers. "He's asleep. The last thing he said was something about an early-morning speed trap on Route 90."

"It's important that I wake him, Martha."

She shrugged and stepped aside. "I only hope you two aren't getting involved in something again."

As he walked through the living room, toward the rear hall, he felt surrounded by the dozens of porcelain figurines perched on every available surface. He wondered, as he often had, how the massive Rocco existed in this suburban china shop.

The sleeping police chief's arms were flung outward as he lightly snored. One eye opened as Lyon shook his shoulder. "Something has happened to Tom Giles."

"You said that earlier."

"He called me from his lake house and said his life was in danger."

"I hope you haven't been into the sherry again." The policeman's eyes blinked open as he swung his legs from the bed and pulled pants over his pajamas. "Tell me about it on the way."

As they drove to the lake house, Lyon told Rocco about Giles's phone call. Rocco looked pensive for a moment. "Then you didn't see his plane go down?"

"Maybe he wasn't in it."

"Are you sure it was Giles who called?"

"Absolutely."

"Then what in hell's going on?" Rocco lapsed into silence as Lyon thought back over their relationship. Although both he and Herbert were from Connecticut, they hadn't met until Korea, where Lyon had served as a divisional intelligence officer and Rocco had been commander of the ranger company. The information obtained by Rocco's probing reconnaissance patrols had brought them into continual contact, and their friendship had deepened after their discharge. The much-decorated Rocco had been offered the job of chief of the Murphysville police force, which sometimes numbered twelve men.

As the car pulled into the cottage drive, Lyon pointed to the dangling phone line swaying before the car's headlights. They entered through the front door, which Lyon had unlocked from inside. Rocco went immediately toward the overturned chair and knelt by the spot on the floor.

"It could be blood."

"You'll get a lab crew out here?"

"For what? We don't know that a crime has been committed."

"Tom has disappeared."

"Has he? We don't know that for sure. You received a phone call, and he wasn't where he said he would be. Hell, he could have been drunk, run off with a girl friend, gone back home . . . anything."

"I think you're wrong," Lyon said, as he began a tour

through the house. A book on the Salem witch trials lay open, face down, on a coffee table. In an ashtray next to it was a pipe with ashes still in the bowl. In the small kitchen, separated from the living room by a bar, he noted a used frying pan on the stove and a plate with silverware in the sink.

It was obvious that the first bedroom had been the one occupied. A man's valise stood in the corner, there were shaving implements in the bathroom medicine chest, and a woman's pants suit was wadded in a corner by the closet. A copy of yesterday's newspaper lay neatly folded on the dresser.

"We had better secure the house and go back to bed," Rocco said from the doorway.

"There isn't anything you can do?"

"Not now. But I'll give Karen Giles a call first thing in the morning."

"Do it now."

"The phone's out."

"When you get home."

"O.K.," he said tiredly. "And if there's anything to report, I'll call you."

Lyon sat on a high kitchen stool and stared into the water bubbling in a saucepan on the stove. He didn't really want instant coffee, and he knew he was merely finding an excuse to stay awake in case Rocco called. His friend's handshake and his mumbled "I don't know" as he walked from the car to his door haunted the last vestiges of the night. As he slid from the stool and reached into the cabinet containing the jar of coffee, the door opened.

"I thought I heard someone in here," Robin said.

"Cup of lousy instant?"

"Please."

He was startled by her appearance as he turned to hand her a cup of coffee. "You sleep in that thing too?"

"The bikini?" She laughed. "I was so tired when we got home that I just fell across the bed. Then, a while ago I thought I heard a car and was wide awake."

"I had to go out for a while."

"I guess I really should take it off." She carefully set her coffee cup on the counter and stood before him as she reached behind her back to undo the bra straps.

"If she takes off a stitch, I'm going to kill her," the soft voice said.

Lyon turned to face Bea. She was wearing her lumpy terrycloth robe and furry rabbit slippers, and her closely cropped hair straggled over her forehead. "Hi, Bea. I hope we didn't wake you?"

"YOU WHAT?"

"I think I'm sleepy again," Robin said and ran for the stairs.

"Tom Giles called and said he was in trouble. Rocco and I went out to his lake house. Well, actually I went first and . . ."

"You aren't for real." She turned and left.

For a moment he looked after his retreating wife, his lips pursed into a low "Oh, boy." Then he bounded up the stairs after her.

She lay huddled on the bed with her face turned toward the wall. "I think I can explain," he said.

Bea turned, plucked the small hearing aid from her ear, and threw it at him. "DON'T BOTHER!"

It was ten A.M. before he was sufficiently awake to go to the study and sit before the typewriter. He looked down at the partially completed manuscript and wondered how the sagacious Danny Dolphin would solve Lyon's marital problem. Robin had come out onto the terrace below the window, spread a blanket, and was sensuously applying suntan oil to her legs. That didn't solve anything, either.

His observations and random thoughts were broken by the phone's ring. She had begun to talk before he had the receiver to his ear. ". . . THE NEXT FLIGHT TO ASHEVILLE! I'll pick up the ticket this afternoon."

"Bea, I want to tell you about what didn't happen."

She gave a long sigh. "I know, Lyon. I trust you. . . . But I'm not so sure about little Robin, girl illustrator."

"She's very talented."

"That's what I'm afraid of."

"Why don't you come home early and we'll go for a long walk?"

"I can't. There's a voter irregularity in Waterburg."

"There are always voter irregularities in Waterburg."

"I'll see you at six."

The phone rang again before his fingers left the receiver. "You were right," Rocco Herbert said in a workaday tone of authority.

Lyon was beginning to wonder why on this morning people were starting conversations in mid-thought. "Right about what?"

"They found the plane this morning. You had better get down to the office right away."

The photograph of the body on the morgue stretcher was of a very dead Tom Giles.

Lyon looked at the picture of his dead friend for a long moment and then slowly handed it back to Rocco. He cleared his throat and turned away. "You said they found his plane."

"With him in it."

"That's impossible."

Lyon pushed back his chair. "Someone flew the plane. Cause of death?"

"He was shot."

"Where?"

"Behind the ear, with a small-caliber handgun."

"Time of death?"

"That's difficult to determine, and the medical examiner wouldn't hazard a guess. It seems that the temperature of the water causes various body changes that are difficult to plot, and that, combined with the fact that no one knows when he last ate or what he ate, makes it impossible for any exact determination of the time of death."

"Which means that he could have been killed at the cottage, in the plane, or almost anywhere else?"

"There's no way to tell."

"Interesting case," Lyon said. "Have fun." He turned to leave but felt Rocco's fingers grip the rear of his shirt.

"You're in this up to your neck."

"No way. Bea would kill me. Come to think of it, she might kill me, anyway."

"Jurisdiction of the case rests with the State Police."

"Let me guess. Your brother-in-law, Captain Norbert."

"He would like to have words with you. He's also a little unhappy about our trip to the Giles cottage last night."

"Which means that they consider me a . . ."

"Suspect? Not a hard one. But Will Barnes and Norbie are curious as to how you could see a plane go down with a dead man in it, and then seventeen hours later get a phone call from the same dead man."

"Corpses don't fly airplanes."

"That's been considered. The divers also brought up a woman's handbag." Rocco handed another large photograph to Lyon. It showed a woman's purse on a black felt background, with the contents of the bag neatly aligned across the bottom of the picture.

Lyon reached for the magnifying glass on the desk and peered through it at the contents of the purse. There was the usual assortment that might be found in any woman's bag: lipstick, mascara, wallet, soggy cigarettes, a silver lighter, some coins and bills, and identification. He read the name on the driver's license: "Carol Dodgson. Have they picked her up?"

"They're still looking for her. The address is a phony."

"She could have floated from the cockpit when the plane went down and been carried away by a current."

"They're still searching."

"Murder weapon?"

"Not in the plane."

"Theories?"

"That Miss Dodgson, as the identification calls her, was involved with Tom Giles. They had a quarrel, she shot him, and she somehow escaped from the plane when it went down."

Lyon looked thoughtful. "That's possible. My visibility was lousy, and I couldn't tell who was in the plane. Did they find it where I said?"

"Five hundred yards to the east. You took a compass reading that was wrong."

"I don't think so."

"You had to. Current couldn't have carried the plane that far."

"What about Tom's wife?"

"I called her last night, as I said I would. She told me he'd been staying at the lake cottage for the past several days."

"That doesn't explain the cut phone wires."

"That doesn't explain anything."

4

Because of an overlapping quirk in Murphysville's zoning maps, Sarge's Bar and Grill was located in a residential area, off a secondary highway. Master Sergeant Renfroe, U.S.A. (Ret.), had been Rocco's "First" during the Korean War and had opted to retire under the protection of his former commanding officer. As Lyon and Rocco entered the dimly lit bar, they found Sarge snoring loudly on a stool behind the bar, with his head buried in his arms, which were folded across the damp wood.

"No more freebies, Willie," Rocco said to the bar's lone customer, who was helping himself to a dusty bottle of Chivas Regal.

"I was gonna settle up, Chief. I really was."

"Uh huh," Rocco said as he propelled the customer out the door, stuck the Closed sign in the window, and locked the door. "Sarge is drinking the profits again. Lyon, why don't you make us a roast beef on rye?"

While Lyon went into the small kitchen beside the bar,

 Rocco pulled the sleeping proprietor erect and let the limp body fall across his shoulders. Easily hefting the unconscious Sarge, he went through a side door and upstairs to the living quarters. By the time he had returned, Lyon had sliced meat, made two sandwiches, and drawn a draft beer for Rocco and a Dry Sack for himself.

"Let me see those pictures again," Lyon said through a mouthful of roast beef.

Rocco handed him the large manila envelope containing the photographs of the dead man and the contents of the purse. "You're on to something?"

Lyon spread the pictures on the table and sipped his sherry. "There's something wrong with these pictures, but I can't get a handle on it."

Three State Police cruisers squealed to a stop in front of the bar, and within moments there was a heavy pounding that rattled the windows. "Christ," Rocco said as he started for the door, "the Lone Ranger is here with his posse."

As the door was unlocked, two trooper corporals stepped inside and peered suspiciously around the interior. They were followed by Captain Norbert, who gave a perfunctory wave to Rocco and strode the length of the bar. "You act like it's a raid, Norbie," Rocco said.

"Hell of a place for a meeting. You just close the place down? Shoulda closed it down a long time ago."

"In a manner of speaking," Rocco replied.

"Where's the suspect?"

"Lyon's in the booth over there, but he isn't a suspect."

"Jesus! Not him again."

"Good to see you again, Captain," Lyon said as he finished a dill pickle.

"All right, Wentworth, what's this crap about a phone call from the deceased?"

"He called me. I'm positive of it."

"As positive as you were about the location of the downed plane? Which just happened to be half a mile in error."

Lyon didn't answer. "The sun was in his eyes," Rocco replied for him.

"And booze in his stomach."

"Wait a minute, Norby. I don't want you browbeating him."

"In the first place, Wentworth, why would the deceased have called you?"

"He told me he felt his life was in danger."

"Why you?"

"I suppose because we went to school together and because he's handled a few legal matters for me and also knew that I'd been involved in the Llewyn murder case."

Captain Norbert cocked a finger at a trooper corporal, who immediately whipped a small pad and pencil from his pocket and stood poised. "What do you know about the deceased?"

Lyon thought a moment. "Old family, Yale law school, and a partner with Saxon, Giles and Hoppelwite in Hartford."

"Don't know them. Must not handle criminal cases."

"Hardly. Corporate law, large real-estate transactions, things of that nature."

"What about his wife?"

"Karen Giles? She's from Washington, a few years younger than Tom, and a very attractive woman. I've met her only a few times, at social functions."

"The phone call could have been a phony."

"I don't think it was, but there's always that possibility. But why?"

"Do you know Carol Dodgson?" the captain snapped.

"The woman in the plane?"

"Yes."

"I had never heard of her until this morning."

"She obviously killed him," Rocco said, "and either

she herself was killed and her body washed away, or she somehow managed to get out of the plane. She killed Giles at the lake house, where we found the blood, and then took the body to the plane."

"What does Giles's wife say about the Dodgson girl?" Lyon asked.

"Never heard of her either. And we can't find her at the ID address. Let's go over the story again, Wentworth. From the beginning."

Lyon recounted the previous day's activities—the balloon ride, the unsuccessful search for the plane, and the night phone call from Giles . . . if it really had been Giles. When he had finished, Norbert tapped his fingers nervously on the edge of the booth.

"You know what I think, Wentworth? I think you're a nut."

Rocco's face hardened. "God damn it! Knock it off, and I don't intend to tell you again!"

"You stay out of this case too, Chief. This matter is under State Police jurisdiction."

"If he was killed at the lake house, it's my case."

As the voices of the two police officers rose in argument, Lyon quietly stood, tucked the envelope of photographs under his arm, and made for the side door.

"There's no proof of where he was killed. And until there is, this is state business."

"Cram the state!" were the last words Lyon heard Rocco say as he slipped out the door and began to walk briskly toward his car.

"OH, MY GOD! HE'S LOOKING AT EVIDENTIAL PHOTOGRAPHS WITH A MAGNIFYING GLASS AGAIN!"

Lyon looked at Bea sheepishly and dropped the magnifying glass. The photographs from Rocco's envelope were spread across a card table he had set up in his study. "You ought to have seen me with aerial photographs of gun emplacements."

"No, Lyon. A thousand times, no." She gathered up the pictures and flipped them into a wastebasket. "You are not working on any murder case. You are not helping your friend out; you are not going to examine snapshots of dead people."

"Tom Giles was a friend and classmate of mine."

"Bull diddle! You've told me a thousand times that Tom was a snob and practically wore a WASP armband."

"Nobody's perfect."

She took an envelope from her pocketbook and slapped it on the table. "One-way ticket to Asheville, North Carolina, on tomorrow's flight. Tourist class."

"Robin and I haven't finished going over the new book for possible illustrations."

"Plane leaves at seven. That gives you all day tomorrow."

"You'll tell her?"

"Oh, no. You tell her. Explain that we're coming down with the plague, or that you've contracted a social disease. Anything."

"That I'm working on a murder investigation."

"Wentworth, that sounds like coercion and extortion."

"Rocco needs help, and, like it or not, I'm apparently some sort of witness. Although I'm not exactly sure what kind."

"What about the new book?"

"I'll work on it tomorrow with Robin, and then spend a day or so with Rocco."

"Only a day or so? Promise?"

"Promise."

She shook her head as she walked slowly to the wastebasket and retrieved the photographs. She spread them back across the table. "And you'll tell Robin?"

"Yes. There's something about this picture of the woman's bag that bothers me."

Bea took the photograph and looked at it intently. "Carol Dodgson—is she the one who killed Giles?"

"We don't know. It just seems odd that she'd commit a crime that was obviously well planned, and then leave her bag in the plane, with her driver's license and Social Security card in it."

"Can't the police find her?"

"No one at that address has ever heard of her."

"She could have panicked when the plane went under water."

"Possibly. There's something else, but I can't put my finger on it."

"There's no mirror."

"What?"

"Look. Here's a woman who supposedly uses lipstick, eye shadow and mascara. Fine, but there's no compact or pocket mirror. Highly unlikely."

"So what does that prove? A missing item. That's what's been bothering me. Too many missing pieces."

"The phone call could have been a recording; the mirror could have been broken that day and not replaced."

"Too much."

Bea looked at the picture again. "I have an idea. Something I can do tomorrow. You're going to work on the book, right?"

"Yes."

"I think I can trace Miss Dodgson."

Halfway to Hartford the next morning, Bea Wentworth decided she was crazy. She had left them together at the breakfast table. As she had leaned over to kiss Lyon good-bye and slap the plane ticket into his palm, the young girl, oblivious to her presence, had stared at Bea's husband over the rim of her coffee cup.

She was crazy. No sane woman would go to work and leave her husband alone in a secluded house with a lovely and infatuated young girl.

She could take the next highway exit, drive back to Nutmeg Hill, leave the car at the end of the drive, and sneak through the woods to . . . No, that was demeaning, and besides, she trusted Lyon implicitly. . . . At least she thought she did.

She pulled the car into the reserved parking place in front of the baroque state capitol and walked briskly to her first-floor office. She smiled and waved at the two secretaries in her anteroom and entered her office.

When she thought of her years in the legislature, fighting against government spending in all areas except social services, she felt a pang of guilt over the opulence of the room. On assuming the position, she had denied herself the customary privilege of redecorating the office. She had stuck with her stand until informed that the unused monies would be utilized for the lieutenant governor's pet project, two slate pool tables in the basement, a sanctuary for male legislators.

The large office had deep powder-blue rugs, damask draperies, and a scowling Kimberly perched on the settee.

"I'm quitting," the black woman said without preamble.

"You said that last week, and I haven't had my coffee yet."

"Doesn't it strike you as paradoxical that, as a revolutionary, I'm spending eight hours a day registering corporations for the state?"

Bea looked at her unhappy friend, whom she had appointed deputy secretary as her first official act. "There's a juicy voting irregularity in Waterburg."

"There are always irregularities in Waterburg."

"You want to go back to organizing the welfare mothers?"

"How'd you guess?"

"Don't you think you can accomplish more by working within the system?"

"That's what you told me last week."

"Before you leave, we have a problem to solve." Bea pulled a sheet of notes from her pocket and spread it on the desk. Kim moved to a side chair and bent over the paper.

"Who's Carol Dodgson?"

"That's what we're going to find out," Bea answered.

"Aren't you awfully hot in that thing?" Lyon asked.

Robin looked up from her sketch pad and felt the neck of the granny dress with one hand. "I could put the bikini back on," she said with a demure smile.

"That's all right," he replied and leaned over the sketch pad. He heard the airline ticket crinkle in his back pocket and reminded himself that he must tell her, perhaps after lunch. The drawing had begun to take shape, and Danny Dolphin's home had become a viable entity. "I like it."

"It's not as good as Dad can do, but I think it captures the flavor of the book. It's a wonderful book, Lyon. It will make every child in America think twice before eating another tuna-fish sandwich."

"Well, now, in Chapter Six, Danny is caught in the tuna nets and . . ." As he continued outlining the book, he felt the pressure of her knee against the side of his leg. He must tell her about the ticket.

"All one hundred and sixty-nine towns?" Kim asked incredulously.

"Every one," Bea replied.

"Suppose this Dodgson woman never voted?"

"Then she never voted. We'll also find out if she was born in Connecticut; went to high school or college here; ever had a telephone, electrical services or a credit rating."

Kim whistled. "That's some job."

"You've got sixty people."

"If the commission on government efficiency catches us doing this, we're all sunk."

"That's what you wanted anyway, isn't it?"

Kim smiled and went to the office door. "All one hundred and sixty-nine towns?"

"And the utilities, and the credit bureaus, and the school systems." When Kim left, Bea reached for the phone and dialed the number of the regional Social Security office.

"Well, that wraps it up," Lyon said as he put the manuscript away in the desk. "You can go back to your dad and begin work on the preliminary drawings, and we might even beat our deadline for once. In fact"—his voice quickened—"why don't you go home tonight? I just happen to have a plane ticket in my pocket."

"She's too old for you," Robin said.

"Bea's a year younger than I am."

"I love you, Lyon. I think you are the most wonderful person I have ever met. I am prepared to dedicate the rest of my life to making you happy. We can be a team; you'll write the books and I'll illustrate them, and we'll keep everything right in the family. After *Danny Dolphin,* we can do the next one together."

"The Wobblies Win."

"Yes, and after that, we can . . ."

He put his finger over her lips, and then his hands on her shoulders. He looked directly at her. "Robin, you know how much I care for you. I think you're a fine person; you have a great deal of talent as an artist, and a whole life ahead of you. But—and this is a very big 'but'—I love my wife. In fact, if I'd been a little precocious, I'm old enough to be your father."

"I don't think of you as a father, Lyon. I don't think of you that way at all."

"Can you tell me when the number 047-66-1979 was issued, to whom, and so forth?" Bea doodled on the pad at her desk as she waited for the Social Security Administration supervisor to pull the file.

"That's a recent issue," the studious voice related. "That series was issued out of this office and sent to a Carol Dodgson less than a month ago."

Bea's confidence sank. The supposition she'd been working on all day faded away. "I see. Can you give me the address where the card was sent?"

"A post-office box in Hartford."

"I see. But wouldn't Miss Dodgson have to go by one of your offices to apply for a card?"

"Not necessarily. It can all be done by mail. There's a form we send out on request, and it takes about six weeks to process a new number."

"Thank you very much." She severed the connection. It was too apparent. A form requested by phone and sent to a box number. Well, there were other contacts to be made. She placed a call to the deputy director of the Motor Vehicle Department, a competent older man who had solicited her support for his appointment. He gave her the information almost immediately.

"That license series comes from a group stolen from the department some months ago. They've been turning up all over the country, usually in the hands of paperhangers."

"Paperhangers?"

"Check forgers. Whoever had that license bought it somewhere. There are a dozen sleazy bars in the state where you can purchase IDs like that."

"Thanks, Harry. 'Preciate it."

"Anytime, Bea. For you, anytime."

Her hands went over his. "I want to go to bed with you."

"You don't mean that. There must be a dozen boys in Round Rock who would be . . ."

"None."

"In fact, speaking of Round Rock, I have a ticket right here."

"I want to make love to you."

Kim stood in the office doorway with a sheaf of papers clutched in each hand. "She's not from this state."

Bea looked up. "Are you sure?"

"Your Miss Dodgson never voted, never had a phone, never had electricity, never went to school and wasn't born here."

"Thanks, Kim. Let's go home."

Her hands left his and went around his neck. He should step back, turn, run. He felt a slight trembling in his legs.

"Will you?" she asked.

"Robin, please . . ."

Her face came closer to his and his arms unconsciously went around her. "Kiss me."

He did.

"Carol Dodgson doesn't exist," Bea said excitedly from the doorway, and then her voice died into silence.

Lyon whirled to face his wife and saw the widening pools of hurt radiating across her face. "Bea, we're working on the book."

"I HOPE THAT WAS THE INTRODUCTION AND NOT THE CONCLUSION!" Bea said, and slammed the door.

5

Bea raced the Datsun's engine and honked the horn impatiently. Lyon leaned against the open car door and stared out over the pines that bracketed the westerly side of the house. He winced as Bea blared the horn in another series of short, staccato blasts.

Robin came out the front door and hitched the backpack over her right shoulder. She wore paint-splattered jeans, a large man's shirt, and sandals. She brushed her hair back from her face and walked slowly to the car.

Before the doors were completely shut, gravel spewed from under the moving car's wheels as it rocked down the drive toward the highway. "How far to Bradley airport?" Robin asked.

"Not far," Bea answered and glanced in the rearview mirror. "Is that your usual traveling outfit?"

"I'm sorry, Beatrice. My crinoline is wrinkled, and the white gloves are dusty."

"Oh, boy," Lyon said under his breath.

"I suppose Lyon and I are of a different generation," Bea said.

"I think some people age faster than others, don't you?"

Lyon cringed back against the headrest as Bea accelerated the car to over seventy.

At the airport security gate, Robin threw her arms around Lyon and kissed him. She formally shook hands with Bea before turning to pass through the arched metal detector and down the ramp toward her flight.

Bea took Lyon's arm and turned him away from the gate. "Come on, lover. There's a murder to investigate—and right now there's nothing I'd like more than a murder investigation."

"Do I detect an emphasis on a particular word?"

The Giles home was a large white colonial with black shutters, off the Murphysville green. On the right-hand side of the second story was a small plaque which read "Circa 1760." As they started up the walk, the front door opened and Cannon Braemer Long bustled out.

He nodded at Bea and Lyon in passing. "Terrible thing. Terrible," he muttered as he turned down the street toward the Holy Trinity Episcopal Church.

Before the chimes had faded away, the front door was opened by a small black woman in a dark uniform and white apron. "Miz Wentworth, Mista' Wentworth."

"Good evening, Hattie. Can we speak with Mrs. Giles?"

"She's in the bed. I'll fetch her. Y'all go in the living room."

"That's the best act since Butterfly McQueen," Lyon said as they walked into the living room.

"Who?"

"The actress who played the hysterical maid in *Gone with the Wind*."

The room was as Lyon had expected. The beamed ceiling, wide hearth with nearby spinning wheel, and the clean functional lines of colonial period furniture created the obvious effect, and yet he had the inchoate feeling that it didn't fit.

The maid stood in the doorway with a handkerchief held to her mouth, which muffled her words. "Miz Giles be down soon."

"Thank you."

As Hattie crossed conspiratorially toward Bea, the handkerchief disappeared somewhere up a sleeve. "Bea, will you be seeing Kim?"

"Yes."

"Please inform her that the literature has arrived from New York and the meeting has been rescheduled for tomorrow evening."

Lyon stared at his wife as the black woman left the room. "What's all that about?"

"I have the feeling that Kim is in the process of organizing a union of domestic workers. I had better see whether she's in violation of the state's little Hatch Act."

"You've begun to turn into a bureaucrat since you got that job." He walked toward the mantelpiece to admire an excellent scale replica of the *Mayflower.* As he did so, one hand brushed against the wall, and he turned to tap lightly against the wallboard. He looked down at his feet, on the edge of a throw rug on the highly waxed flooring.

Several years before, the Wentworths had purchased the decrepit house on the promontory and named it Nutmeg Hill. Room by room, as their finances allowed, they had restored the structure. Each peg, each section of plaster, had become as familiar to Lyon as his own face in the morning mirror.

This house was not of that ilk. In fact, nothing in the house was as it seemed: from a caricature of a maid who dropped her obsequiousness at will, to plasterboard walls and floor planking laid closer to 1960 than to 1760. He ran his fingers along the under edge of the cobbler's bench coffee table and felt machine-milled nails and belt-sanded wood. Not only the house but also the furniture and probably the plaque on the outside wall were reproductions . . . the ultimate compromise between a sense of history and old Yankee frugality.

"Beatrice," the soft voice said from the doorway. "How good of you to come." Karen Giles extended both hands as she moved across the room toward Bea.

She was a tall woman, dressed in black, with her blond hair pulled back in a severe bun. The simplicity of the hair style seemed to accentuate her perfectly proportioned facial features. She moved with a flowing, athletic stride, with just the proper hint of sexuality to her hips. The early thirties would be her approximate age, Lyon thought.

"We were sorry to hear of your loss," Bea said.

"Thank you for your thoughts." She turned to Lyon and held out a hand, her voice small and lilting. "Thank you also, Lyon."

The dampness of her palm belied her apparent composure. "If there's anything we can do?"

"Thank you, nothing. The services will be in a few days, but I can't really make any definite announcement until the police release the . . ." Her hands went to her face as her shoulders momentarily shook; then her composure returned. "Perhaps some sherry?"

"That would be nice."

Karen poured small measures of sherry from a cut-glass decanter on a sideboard and handed the glasses to the Wentworths. "Have you heard anything about that woman? The one who killed Tom? Have they caught her yet?"

"There isn't any such person as Carol Dodgson," Bea said.

"I don't understand."

"The handbag in the airplane was a plant. Every attempt I made to trace the Dodgson woman turned up absolutely nothing."

"Then someone else murdered Tom?"

"Exactly," Lyon said.

Karen Giles sat back on the sofa, crossed her legs, sipped her sherry quickly, and then laughed. "I should have known. Tom would never play around. It didn't fit his image."

"The police have assumed that Tom went to the lake house to be alone with the Dodgson woman, there was an argument, and she killed him. But that doesn't seem to be the case now."

Karen went to the sideboard and poured another sherry. "No, it doesn't."

"Why *was* he out there?" Lyon asked.

She shrugged. "Tom liked to get away once in a while, to work on briefs or just to be alone."

Lyon had first recognized the impulse as an intelligence officer during the Korean War, when bits and pieces of seemingly unrelated information had been channeled across his field desk. He had learned to follow the instinctual, almost subliminal leaps of logic from random parts to a logical whole. "Have the divorce papers been filed yet?"

Karen Giles turned toward him with a blank stare, and he noticed how blue her eyes were. "I don't know."

The jump had been made, and he'd have to press it home. "The file will turn up at court, or there'll be copies of the documents at his office."

She continued staring at him for long moments before speaking. "I suppose they will."

"What were the grounds?"

"Irreconcilable differences. He wouldn't have it any other way. You ought to know that, Lyon. Form and appearance were terribly important to Tom. To finish answering your question, Tom was filing on Monday. That's why he was at the lake house."

"That's all."

"That's all you're going to get." Her voice had changed; the lilting boarding-school affectation had disappeared, to be replaced by a hard, cutting quality. "Screw the sherry. I'm going to have a whiskey. Anybody want one?" They shook their heads as she mixed a stiff drink at the sideboard. "Shall I let it all hang out?"

"If you want."

"The police didn't pick up the divorce thing or that I've been taking flying lessons. And there is some money involved. Term insurance, of course; Tom was too cheap to buy anything else. Let me see, there's about a hundred thousand of that, and then the law firm will pay me something for his partnership. There're the houses, mortgaged, but with something left over. Oh, I've made my calculations; say, a quarter of a million all told. Enough so that I don't have to take to the streets."

"Where were you the . . . " Lyon was momentarily perplexed. He didn't know whether it was the day or night of the murder. "The time of the murder?"

"Flying lessons."

"Day or night?"

"Night. Ground school. You know, learning about radios, flight plans, all that."

"And during that day?"

"Right here—home."

"Where were the ground-school lessons given?"

"At the airport where Tom kept the plane."

"With a net worth of a quarter of a million, at least Tom didn't have any financial worries," Bea said.

"Ha! A façade," Karen Giles said. "Tom drew forty-two thousand dollars a year from the firm. Do a little arithmetic. This house costs eight hundred a month to carry, not including the maid, club dues and his airplane. We skirted on the verge of financial insolvency."

"All that money . . . "

"What money? Term insurance he couldn't borrow on, his interest in the firm, property he couldn't sell; we were more and more in debt every year. Then recently he's been taking out notes with every bank in town. God only knows why, or how much the interest payments ran each month. He was always scheming, saying that he had a financial killing around the corner. Some big deal in the wind, but I never saw any of it."

"Family money?" Lyon asked.

"You've got to be kidding! Old man Giles was a custodian at the Breeland High School, and Tom's mother was a bank teller. They're both dead now, and Tom had to pay the funeral expenses."

"Tom and I went to Greenfield Prep together, and then to Yale."

"Sure. An only child who his family sacrificed for and who got good scholarships. I never said Tom wasn't bright. Fooled you, didn't he? Fooled me, too, when we married."

"How's that?" Lyon asked.

"We met in Washington when Tom was appointed to some sort of committee. One of those prestigious things with hardly any salary. I bought the 'old family' bit, too. At first he talked about the possibility of becoming a presidential aide or counsel, and then after Watergate, when those jobs weren't so desirable, he wanted to return to Hartford with the proper wife: the Washington socialite with the proper voice, walk and looks—with vague references to my father the senator. That was all to clinch the partnership with the firm."

"Who was your father?"

"Frank McMann. He was a senator, all right—sold hot

 dogs at the ball park for the Washington Senators. I was as phony as Tom—airline stewardess, a little drama school, and part-time cocktail waitress. I'm a reproduction, Wentworths, just like the house and Tom's life. If you can't have the real thing, manufacture it. That's the compromising legal mind for you. And I was the compromise for the woman he didn't get."

"About the divorce?"

"Screw you," she said sweetly, with a return of affectation.

"You know," Lyon said to Bea when they were back in the car and driving away from the house on the green, "I would have liked the poor bastard better if I had known who he really was."

"You knew him as he really was."

"I suppose."

"Well, you've got a number-one suspect in Mrs. Thomas Giles. Motive: the divorce and money. She flies, and her alibi is probably weak. Also, there's more to that whole divorce bit. And did you notice another thing?"

"What's that?"

"Karen Giles has had a face lift."

"How could you tell?"

"Little line behind the ear."

"Christ, that too?"

"You've probably got more than Rocco or the State Police. When are you going to call them?"

"After I speak to the owner of the airport about Karen's lessons, and learn a little more about Tom's plane and when it left."

"Then Rocco and Norbert take it from there."

"I guess," Lyon replied, lost in thought. He wondered what sort of financial dealings Tom Giles had been involved in, and with whom. There was always the possibility he had been playing games with trust funds at the law office . . . but the police would check that out.

The Murphysville airport was a modest one. A dozen small planes were tied and chocked along the grassy edge of its single runway. It had two hangars and a small, unpainted operations office. The complex was dark as they turned into the parking area.

"Over there," Bea said, and pointed to a lone light burning in a small A-frame a hundred yards to the rear of the operations office.

The man who opened the A-frame's door looked like a dissipated young Lindbergh. Tousled hair stuck out from under a greasy fifty-mission hat crushed to the top of his head. He leaned against the door and gave them an out-of-focus smile. "Sorry, folks, field's socked in." He peered into the darkness. "I'll be damned. It's night already."

"We're looking for the field manager," Lyon said.

The man in the fifty-mission hat bowed, lurched, and grasped the door frame for support. "Gary Middleton at your service—manager, owner, instructor, and chief mechanic."

"I'd like to discuss housing my aircraft here."

"Ah, a paying customer. You are welcome, sir. Come in."

They entered the small house, which seemed to consist of a living room, with a battered divan and a coffee table covered with flying magazines; a kitchen; and a back bedroom. In the corner stood a small desk, with a rather large pile of invoices and bills lying next to an open checkbook and a half-empty bottle of vodka. Through the open bedroom door they could see a king-size bed. Lyon sat next to Middleton on the couch, while behind them Bea moved surreptitiously toward the desk and the checkbook and bills.

"We have hangar facilities or open tie-down. What do you fly?"

Lyon brushed his hair back with a casual hand. "Well, it's about sixty-eight feet long."

"My God, what's the wingspan?"

"That's not exactly the term, but the circumference is about sixty-four feet."

"Hot damn!" Gary Middleton stood up and threw his hat to the floor. "You've got a World War Two B-17."

"More like a toy that got out of hand," Bea said from the desk, as she flipped through the checkbook.

"One of those crazy stunt planes?"

"Not exactly, although I have taken it up to 15,000 feet."

Gary Middleton's face fell. "I hope you're not one of those hot-air nuts. There's one menace around here who floats around in a balloon with a monster face painted all over the side. First time I saw it, I damn near crashed into a radio transmission tower."

"Was Karen Giles with you last night?"

The pilot's face drained as he stood up, with a rush of sobriety. "What is this? You some sort of cop?"

"No, just an interested party."

"I've already talked to the police, so get out!"

Bea sat demurely in a folding chair and smiled at the field manager. "Mr. Middleton is upset because his business is on the verge of bankruptcy."

"Did you tell that to the authorities?" Lyon asked.

"I know you; you're that Wentworth who gets mixed up with that big son of a bitch Rocco Herbert."

"What about the business?" Bea pressed.

"In other words, if I don't talk to you, those damn state and local cops descend on the field like a horde of locusts. Four cars, yet. Christ!"

"I'll personally see that Rocco comes back tomorrow."

"All right, all right. To answer both questions, yes, Karen Giles was here last night, and the field is financially in lousy shape."

"Where did you give her lessons and for how long?"

"Right here. Well, in there." He jerked his thumb toward the bedroom.

“Did Mrs. Giles say she’d put money into the business?”

“I asked her for about thirty thou; that would take me over the hump. She left about midnight.”

“How long have you and Karen been having these private night lessons?”

“Couple of months. It’s not all screwing; sometimes we talk flying.”

“How proficient a flyer is she?”

“Soloed a month ago. She’s ready for her license.”

“Did you see Tom Giles take off?”

“Sure. I saw him go up. The day before yesterday. I was standing here in the window and saw him take off.”

“You’re sure it was Giles?”

“Of course I’m sure. It was his plane. He called me and told me to top the tanks and have it at the end of the runway for an afternoon takeoff.”

“And you saw him actually get in the plane?”

“No, not really, but I saw it taxi to the runway and make a takeoff.”

“Then you’re not positive that Tom Giles was in the plane?”

“Well, I suppose not. But who else would it be?”

“Weren’t you disturbed when he took off and never came back?”

“Not particularly. He often took cross-country hops on the weekend.”

“Without a flight plan?”

“We’re casual here.”

“Thanks for the help,” Lyon said as they started for the door.

“Hey, you’ll keep Herbert off my back, won’t you? All those cop cars pulling onto the field make visitors think we’ve had a crash or something. Scares the hell out of people.”

“I’ll try,” Lyon replied.

Bea was pensive as they drove home. "How bad is his financial condition?" Lyon asked.

"Overdrawn at the bank, and the creditors are ready to foreclose. A quick guess would be that he'll be in bankruptcy court before the month is out. It all fits. Gary Middleton and Karen Giles were having an affair; he needs money; and the only way she can get her hands on any is through her husband's death."

"And Middleton says that Giles's plane took off in the afternoon, yet I didn't see it until the following morning."

"Or, in the police version, until hours after that."

"Of course, someone else could have taken the plane and landed it somewhere else, at another field."

"Or Middleton could be lying."

He drove rapidly through the night. In the past, Lyon had always felt that any problem was soluble; that with a consistent and logical input of facts, logical conclusions could be drawn. At the present time, he wasn't sure what was true and what wasn't.

"Look at that hitchhiker on this desolate road," Bea said.

"The new generation," he said with a smile at his wife as he braked the car to a halt. He reached toward the rear door and snapped the lock up. "Hop in. We can give you a lift a little way up the . . ."

"I have my sleeping bag, and I can crash on the barn floor," Robin said as she swung into the car. "I won't be a bit of trouble."

The car accelerated toward Nutmeg Hill, and Lyon wondered how long Bea could hold her breath like that.

6

“There’s a convoy coming up the drive,” Kim said from the breakfast-nook window. “I think we’re being raided.”

Lyon and Bea craned to see the road from the window. Two State Police cars, followed by Rocco’s Murphysville cruiser, drove up in front of the house and ground to a halt. A phalanx of uniformed men stalked toward the door, the ever-present duo of corporals in the lead, then Captain Norbert, and a trailing Rocco Herbert. “Do we have enough coffee?” Lyon asked as the door knocker began an impatient thunk.

“I’ll lace it with a little ground glass,” Kim grumbled.

Lyon tightened his bathrobe, ran a hand across his shock of falling hair, and padded in bare feet toward the door.

The corporals and the captain were immaculate in their knife-creased trousers and wide-brimmed hats, while Rocco looked sheepish and apologetic in rumpled khakis. The early arrival of the authorities disconcerted Lyon. A vague twinge of puritan guilt made him momentarily want to confess to a hundred unknown crimes in order to gain their approbation. He gestured into the house. "There's coffee in the kitchen."

"I told you to lay off, Wentworth," Norbert said as they followed him through the house.

Kim grimaced as the four officers overflowed the breakfast nook, while Bea poured more mugs of coffee. "Who's she?" one of the corporals asked, with a gesture toward the black woman. "The maid?"

Kim's mouth gaped, Rocco rolled his eyes toward the ceiling, and Bea stiffened. "Ms. Ward happens to be deputy secretary of the state," Bea said icily. "In the state hierarchy, that's the equivalent of police major, Corporal."

The trooper reddened and stared intently into the depths of his coffee mug.

"I'm here to give you a final warning," Norbert said. "We will not tolerate your interviewing witnesses." As Bea purposely cleared her throat, the captain seemed to dwell momentarily on her state position. "That is to say, we'd rather you didn't get involved, sir."

"I was going to call Rocco as soon as I finished my coffee."

"Untrained civilian involvement only complicates our job."

"What did you find out?" Rocco asked with interest.

"Karen and Tom Giles were filing for divorce; Karen is having an affair with Gary Middleton; and there's no proof that Giles flew the plane."

"We were going over that ground again this morning."

"Did you turn up anything at the lake cottage?"

"The blood spot near the telephone table matched

with Giles's type. We're still convinced that the call you claim to have received was a hoax."

"There's no way to trace a local call made within the town limits," Rocco said.

Robin entered the kitchen through the back door. "Hey, what is this? A raid?"

The two small boys fishing at the end of the Lantern City town pier looked at Lyon with interest as he spread the balloon envelope and prepared the propane burner for ignition.

"What's that thing, mister?"

"A hot-air balloon. If you'll give me a hand you can have a ride." The addition of four small hands helped speed up the preparations, and in twenty minutes the balloon had filled and the bag was bobbing over the basket. Lyon climbed into the gondola and swung the boys in beside him. As he began his preflight check, a police car drove onto the dock and stopped with a screech of brakes.

"What in hell's going on?" Chief Barnes yelled from the car window.

"Glad you're here, Barnes. Can you tell me exactly where the plane was found?"

"You'll be able to see the red marker buoy when you're aloft. Wait a minute! Get out of that thing and empty out whatever it is you fill it with."

"Hot air, Chief."

"Don't be smart, Wentworth. There's an ordinance against what you're doing."

"A law against launching a balloon from the town dock?" Lyon gave the burner a five-second ignition. The loud whoosh of flame startled Barnes, and he drew back from the car window. The balloon quickly rose as the small boys gaily waved.

"Hey, this is neat-o, mister!"

Lyon nodded and tried to remember at what altitude he had been flying that morning. He decided to compromise at six hundred feet. It was a windless day, and drift was minimal. As he leveled the balloon, he looked seaward for the distant marker buoy.

He distinctly recalled having given a 170 bearing over the radio. He took a reading from the small pocket compass. It was unmistakable. The buoy lay 190 degrees off the town dock.

Lyon threw the switch underneath the carriage, and the hum of the electric typewriter immediately ceased. Danny Dolphin was becoming hopelessly confused. The morning's balloon trip at Lantern City had only complicated the situation, and now further progress with his naïve dolphin had become impossible.

"You try to keep them in the barn and they come through the front door," Bea said from the hall.

"What are you talking about?"

"Girls. Girls with hardly any clothes on. The bereaved widow has shucked mourning black for more attractive attire." She opened the door to admit Karen Giles, dressed in a brief tennis dress with ruffled panties.

"I'm in trouble, Lyon, and I need your help."

Her hands began to steady after the second sherry. Lyon could envision his imaginary dolphin snorting with a disgusted flip of his tail and heading downstream toward the sea.

"I don't believe I've ever seen a stuffed toy that big," Karen said with an echo of her youthful tone.

The six-foot Wobbly doll stood in the corner by the fireplace, with a nonchalant paw on the mantel. "He's loyal and can keep a confidence," Lyon said. He looked at her, huddled on the leather chair, grasping the glass with both hands. "You said you were in trouble."

“The police were back this morning. They kept pressing, asking me all sorts of questions about our life together and the divorce.”

“I told them. They would have found out sooner or later.”

“When I went to the club after they left, one of them followed me.”

“It stands to reason that when a husband is murdered, they are going to look at the wife very carefully.”

“It’s more than a look. I think they consider me a suspect.”

“What do you want me to do?”

“Make them leave me alone.”

“Rocco and I are good friends, but the case is being handled by the State Police.”

“I could retain you.”

“I’d be breaking some law or other.” Lyon looked out the window and down toward the river below. In the distance, a canoe with two occupants held to the main current of the stream.

It was a distant memory. *“Come on, Went! For Chris’ sake, don’t twist the paddle—in and out, in and out.”* The canoe turned a bend in the river and was lost from view.

He turned back to Karen Giles. “I suppose I’m already indirectly involved. I’d like to see the discrepancies cleared up. Have you talked to Gary Middleton since Sunday?”

“I was going to get to that. I called him this morning, and while we were on the phone the police arrived to take him to the barracks. You know about Gary and me?”

Lyon nodded. “When Bea and I talked with you, you mentioned that Tom was involved in some large financial transaction, that he’d been borrowing money to invest. Do you know any of the details?”

“No, not really. Recently Tom hadn’t kept me

 informed about his business transactions. I know only that it was something on his own and not with the firm, and that he was involved with someone else."

"Who?"

"I don't know, except that he was scared to death his partner was somehow going to do him out of his share."

"How's that?"

"He made a remark one night. He said he knew Esposito was going to screw him; it was just a question of how and when."

"Who's Esposito?"

"I don't know."

The far wing of the house had once been intended for use as a playroom and still housed a Ping-Pong table. At the beginning of her political career, Bea had begun to utilize it as her headquarters. As a consequence, the table was covered with hundreds of copies of legislative bills, and along one wall were stored her most prized possessions—coded three-by-five file cards on all the voters in her senatorial district. As well as Lyon could remember, the code ran from 1—extremely favorable toward Beatrice Wentworth, will contribute and work on campaign—to 7—get rid of that crazy broad.

Along another wall was a long bookcase stuffed with political reference works and telephone books. Lyon cleared a place on the Ping-Pong table and pulled out the phone books to look up all the Espositos.

One hundred forty-three Espositos were listed in the upper portion of the state. Lyon sighed and penciled on a scratch pad the few sentences he would use on each phone call.

On the ninety-third call a voice answered, "Esposito Enterprises."

"Mr. Esposito, please. It's urgent."

The guttural voice announced simply, "E. here."

"Before he died, Tom Giles assigned his interest to me."

There was a long pause on the other end of the line, and Lyon waited apprehensively for the puzzled questioning he had been getting on the other calls. "I see," the voice of Esposito finally said. "And just what do you expect me to do?"

"I think we should meet as soon as possible."

"Who is this?"

"Lyon Wentworth."

"I will expect you at my home this evening, Mr. Wentworth. The address is 711 Braeland Drive, Tallman. Shall we say eight?"

"I'll be there," Lyon said as the connection was severed. He tried to reconstruct the few sentences of the phone call in order to discover what had been said or what innuendo had been made that filled him with such a sense of menace.

"ALL RIGHT, WENTWORTH! I'VE DECIDED WHAT TO DO ABOUT ALL THESE WOMEN!"

Lyon turned to face Bea in the doorway. "Tie Robin to the wing of the plane."

"Not exactly."

"I never knew you went to bed so early," Rocco said to the robed Lyon as they hunched over coffee in the study.

"I think it's called preventive medicine."

"How's that?"

"Never mind. What do you know about an Esposito Enterprises in Tallman?"

"Why?"

"I'll fill you in later. Have you ever heard of them?"

"No, but I could call Pat Pasquale over there and see if he has anything on them. By the way, we had Gary

 Middleton at the barracks all afternoon. He took a polygraph."

"How'd it turn out?"

"Christ, I don't know. The bastard lies about everything. For God's sake, we even got a spike when we asked him his name."

"I imagine Gary and Karen head Norbert's list."

"And mine too, unless you've come up with something."

"Call Pat and see if he has anything on Esposito."

Rocco dialed the Tallman police and asked to speak to Sergeant Pat Pasquale. "Pasquale, you wop bastard, how much did you make off the pad this week? . . . Rocco Herbert here. . . . Sure I can; I'm half myself. Listen, Pat. You ever hear of an outfit called Esposito Enterprises? . . . Uh huh, what do you have on them?" As Rocco listened, he flipped a pad out, cradled the phone between his ear and shoulder and made hasty notes. "Thanks, Pat. See you."

"Well?" Lyon asked.

"Sal Esposito owns a chain of massage parlors, porno book stores, and a couple of bars with exotic dancers. He's been busted six or seven times, all nolles."

"That sounds like syndicate stuff. I'm surprised he's not into book."

"Pat suspects that he's the local layoff bank."

"I think I'd like you with me in mufti when I meet with Mr. E. tonight."

"What did you tell him?"

"That Tom Giles assigned his business interest in the transaction to me."

"Christ, that's a good way to get yourself killed!"

"That's why I want you along."

"You know, of course, that I can get in a sling over this. I'm limited because this is out of my jurisdiction. Norbert will have my—"

"What did you say?" Lyon interrupted excitedly.

"Esposito lives out of my jurisdiction."

"No. 'Limited.' You said 'limited'—limited service."

"What in hell are you talking about?"

"What's the day today?"

"If you were a working man like the rest of us, old buddy, you'd have the date engraved on your heart. . . . It's the first—payday."

"And the plane went down on Sunday the thirtieth."

"Or Monday morning the thirty-first."

"The phone call from the lake house came after midnight Sunday—on the thirty-first. Damn! Let's go to the phone company."

"You can't trace a local call."

"We'll see, Rocco. Let's go down to the phone company and talk to the night supervisor."

"One problem, Lyon."

"What's that?"

"Don't you think you should put some clothes on first?"

Terrance Ralston, night supervisor of the Murphysville phone office, smiled and shook hands. "I'm sorry, Chief Herbert. Ma Bell can do a lot of things, but we don't keep records on local calls. Sometimes the subscriber will request it for business reasons of some sort, and we can attach a monitor to the line for counts, but that's about it."

"Limited service," Lyon said.

"I told you it couldn't be done," Rocco said. "This is a waste of time."

"Yes," the supervisor said. "If the subscriber was on limited service, we'd have a count for the billing period."

Rocco turned to face the still-smiling supervisor. "What's that?"

"People who own vacation homes, or retired people

 on small incomes, often have limited service. It costs less, and the phone's there if they need it," Lyon said.

"That's right," the supervisor agreed. "The monthly base rate is half the regular rate, but you get only thirty free local calls a month; after that we charge twelve and a half cents per call."

"The Murphysville billing period is the thirtieth of each month, and the phone at the Giles lake house was cut by the time you got there. Which means that there was only the period from midnight until the time the line was cut that someone could have made a call on the lake-house phone, and that one call should appear on the register."

"I'll be right back," the supervisor said.

In five minutes they had proof from the phone company that a call had gone out from the Giles lake house between midnight and two.

"That still doesn't prove that it was Giles calling you," Rocco said. "Hell, it could have been someone ordering pizza."

"It was Giles," Lyon said. "But I still haven't figured out how."

7

"I wonder when he's going to finish the house," Rocco said as he pulled the car to a halt in front of 711 Braeland.

A distant streetlight partially illuminated the long, low white building that stretched along the secluded lane. A high wall enclosing the backyard hid the rear portion of the house. The building's flat roof gave it an uncompleted look, as if the second story had been forgotten. Long rectangular windows periodically broke the building's front surface.

Lyon shrugged and stepped from the car. "Doesn't look like anyone's home, but let's try it."

As they strode up the walk to the front door, Rocco put his arm on his friend's shoulder. "Listen, let me handle this. This Esposito's been in the rackets since he was a kid, and he's going to be a real hard ass." He unconsciously shifted the weight of the small .38 in its spring holster under his civilian jacket.

"Let me play along with my Giles bit for a while."

"See what good it does you, then I'll take over."

Lyon pressed a small recessed doorbell. From the depths of the house they heard a deep musical tone. In moments the door was opened by a bowing Japanese.

Lyon returned the bow. "Mr. Wentworth to see Mr. Esposito." They were waved inside with a gesture toward a low shoe rack. The Japanese silently disappeared through a sliding panel at the rear of the vestibule.

"What in hell is this?" Rocco asked as Lyon slipped out of his sneakers and placed them carefully in the shoe rack.

"I think your hood Esposito has an interest in Japanese culture. You're supposed to remove your shoes."

Rocco grunted as he pulled off his shoes and placed them beside Lyon's. His 14Ds dwarfed the sneakers. "A Japanese butler, yet. I thought all those guys left to become sales managers of electronics companies."

"Uh huh," Lyon replied as he stood before a figure-design print on the wall. "Edo period, I should think. Perhaps even an original Utamaro."

"It is, Mr. Wentworth. Very perceptive." Esposito had noiselessly appeared through a sliding panel and now stood with his arms folded inside his exquisitely embroidered kimono. "You know a little of Japanese culture?" The considerable bulk of the man was only slightly concealed by the loose folds of the kimono. The heavily jowled face drooped under closely cropped hair.

"A little. I had occasion to pass through on my way to Chosen."

"Ah, yes. Korea."

"The rest of us called it FECOM," Rocco said.

Esposito looked toward the chief and then back to Lyon.

"My associate, Mr. Herbert," Lyon said.

Esposito bowed. "Yes, we all must have associates. Do come in for tea, gentlemen." He led the way through the panel into a series of rooms decorated in Japanese style. At the rear of the house he stopped before a low table.

"A perfect example of a *shoin,*" Lyon said as he began to examine a shelf of books next to the long windowsill.

"Yes, a writing room. Perhaps you would like to see the garden?"

"I would be honored." Esposito pressed a small panel above the windowsill, and floodlights immediately illuminated the walled garden at the rear of the house. The area, perhaps a quarter of an acre, was covered with pure white sand raked in concentric circles around a composition of black rocks. "I saw a *hira-niwa* like this at the Ronji Temple," Lyon said.

"An exact duplicate." Esposito sat cross-legged on the *tatami.* Rocco looked decidedly uncomfortable as he twisted his legs from one position to another at the low table. Tea was unobtrusively served.

"I am not unaware of you, Mr. Wentworth. You're one of our local authors. Children's literature, I believe."

"Yes, *The Cat in the Capitol,* the Wobbly series; I'm working on a dolphin story at the moment."

"Ah, admirable. I work with the *haiku* myself. In Japanese, of course."

"Of course."

"I understand you own a string of porn shops and flesh rubs," Rocco said abruptly.

"You have the impatience of the Occidental, Mr. Herbert. Yes, I am the proprietor of what I prefer to call houses of illusion."

"A Japanese Esposito?" Rocco asked.

"I am of Italian heritage, Mr. Herbert. To be more exact, Sicilian. I find that an interest in Oriental culture is a diversion from the exigencies of day-to-day business."

"I'll bet."

Esposito turned from Rocco. "I can only assume, Mr. Wentworth, that your associate Mr. Herbert has been brought along as what certain of my associates would call insurance."

"In a manner of speaking."

"Interesting. It might be educational to pit him against Mr. Koyota, the gentleman who ushered you in. Mr. Koyota is half Mr. Herbert's size, but highly trained in the martial arts. He's of samurai lineage."

"About my acquisition of Mr. Giles's interest in the venture . . ."

"Yes. Most interesting, your obtaining that. Perhaps Mr. Herbert was persuasive, or did Mr. Herbert remove the problem?"

"I don't think I care for that implication," Rocco said.

"It was ungracious of me," Esposito said, as Koyota silently entered and slipped him a note. He glanced down at the slip of paper for a moment and then up at Lyon. "Mr. Wentworth, I see your wife is our secretary of the state. I should have put the two names in apposition. You did not identify yourself as a police authority, Mr. Herbert. Or should I say Chief Herbert?"

"We didn't think it was necessary," Lyon said.

Esposito stood. "I believe I would rather talk to Mr. Wentworth alone, Chief Herbert. From unfortunate prior experience, I find business discussions in the presence of police officials most unpleasant."

"I can imagine," Rocco replied.

"It's all right, Rocco. I'll be back in a few minutes." Lyon followed the robed man through a sliding panel into a large room containing a solarium roof and a glistening swimming pool.

"You may join me if you wish, Mr. Wentworth." He carefully folded the kimono and laid it on a teakwood bench. He stepped from the side of the pool and sank into the warm water. He immediately bobbed to the surface and hovered there with slight motions of his arms. "Mr. Giles's portion of the endeavor was not assignable. He, more than anyone else, would know that."

"He's not around to amplify on the situation, Mr. Esposito."

"Yes; a pity. He drew up the papers himself, structured it in such a way that it actually became a tontine."

"I didn't know they were still legal."

"For all his other faults, Mr. Giles was an excellent attorney. But I'm afraid I can't go into further detail." He swam lazily along the length of the pool as Lyon walked the edge.

"If I understand the term, upon the death of one or more members of a tontine, the remaining shares go to the survivors."

"A convenient arrangement."

"What's the transaction?"

"Please, Mr. Wentworth. Business details of that nature must be kept in strict confidence. However, I can tell you that it is completely legal."

"How many other partners are there?"

"More than myself, let me assure you."

"It does give you a motive, doesn't it, Mr. Esposito?" With outstretched arms the bulky man began to float on his back. "Yes, doesn't it?"

The study was crowded, which made it difficult for Lyon to pretend not to hear Rocco's conversation with his wife. Lyon had wheeled a bar cart into the room to mix drinks. He poured a jigger of vodka for Rocco.

"Yes, dear," Rocco mumbled into the phone as he kept his back turned from the others in the room. "I know I don't get overtime, but it's a murder investigation. . . . At Lyon's house. . . . Kim and Robin. . . . I know they're not on the force. . . . "

Lyon poured a second shot into Rocco's drink.

"I know your brother's working on the case, but . . . "

On further thought, Lyon decided that three would relax Rocco even more, and he poured it heavy.

The large police officer replaced the phone on the cradle, mopped his brow, and turned to the others with officious authority. "All right, let's get to work."

"I think it's exciting," Robin said as she sat cross-legged on the floor against the blackboard propped next to the Wobbly doll.

Bea glowered.

Lyon passed drinks around, tossed his off, and went to the blackboard. "O.K., we have three sets of suspects: Karen Giles and her pilot lover; Sal Esposito; and the other members of the tontine." Everyone shivered as he wrote the names with squeaking chalk.

Kim jumped to her feet. "I can write more legibly."

"The State Police are over Karen Giles like a tent," Rocco said. "I'll check out Esposito's alibi, if he has one, with Hartford."

Lyon sat on the edge of the desk and stared at the blackboard and at the large map tacked over the fireplace. He knew it was an open-ended problem, beginning with the business tontine, however that was arranged, and ending with Giles's murder—however *that* was arranged. It could be attacked from either direction, and preferably from both simultaneously.

"I was with Norbert when they went through Giles's papers," Rocco said. "I didn't see anything out of the ordinary."

"Now that we know he was involved with Esposito, will you double-check it?"

"Right."

"It would seem to me," Bea said, "that if we knew when and how the murder was committed, we might have something to go on."

"Exactly," Lyon responded and took the chalk from Kim, who shook her head and retreated to her drink. "I saw a plane go down in the sound in the morning. The plane was not found until the following day—in a different location. There are several possibilities." He began to list them on the board.

"I didn't really see the plane go down in the morning."

"How much sherry have you had, Wentworth?" Bea asked.

"Dr. Rhine did some interesting work on extrasensory perception at Duke," Robin said.

Bea sniffed. "With missing airplanes?"

"I think it was marks on cards."

"Two: I saw an entirely different airplane."

"It was never found."

Lyon drew a line through the second alternative. "Which brings me to the third possibility: the plane went down when I saw it, but Giles wasn't in it."

"Someone killed Giles later, and then placed the body in the plane—which would explain the phone call."

"A strong possibility," Lyon said.

"Wait a minute, Lyon," Bea said. "You said you were positive of the compass bearing when you saw the plane go down."

"The compass could have been tampered with," Kim said. "Wasn't it stolen from the beach?"

"Yes, it was. And unless the police in Lantern City can locate the stuff that was ripped off, there's no way to tell how accurate the reading was. Then there's the time problem concerning when the plane took off."

"The killer could have flown it to another airport and then taken it up again later," Robin said.

Bea looked hopeful. "That should be checked out."

Lyon drew a circle on the map. "The murderer had to land the plane, kill Giles at the lake house, move the body, and then fly into the water and escape. He had to keep the plane either in Connecticut, lower Massachusetts, or Rhode Island."

"What about Long Island?"

"Couldn't get over there and back fast enough."

"I could check out the airports," Robin said. "There can't be more than thirty or forty in that circle."

"That's a great idea," Bea said. "Take the pickup and drive very slowly."

The early visitor to Nutmeg Hill stood planted on the front stoop. The black Cadillac in the driveway behind him matched the color of his suit, although some lighter material woven into the fabric gave it an iridescent quality. Lyon wondered whether it was to be magazine subscriptions or aluminum siding. He ruled out magazines because of the Caddy and replaced them with Food Freezer Plan. He smiled. "Yes?"

"You Wentworth?"

"Yes," Lyon replied, although he didn't consider the question the best opening remark for a door-to-door salesman.

"E. sent me. He wants you should steep yourself in the culture of the land of Nippon."

"Tell Mr. Esposito that it's an area of great interest to me, and sometime again I may take a trip to the Orient."

"E. says *now.*"

"What?"

An extended finger poked Lyon in the sternum. He involuntarily stepped backward. The man followed him into the hallway, reached into his breast pocket for an

oblong envelope, and jammed it into Lyon's hand. "E.
says he's worried about crime in the streets and wants you should go to Japan . . . tonight."

Lyon opened the envelope and saw the airline tickets: Hartford to San Francisco to Hawaii to Tokyo—one way.

"E. says he'll send you return tickets in three months."

"Well, that's very nice of Mr. Esposito, but I really couldn't take . . . "

"Don't be funny, Wentworth. E. isn't asking; he's telling."

"It's not convenient for me to fly to Japan tonight."

"Like I say, E. is worried about street crime. He's taken a liking to you and don't want you should accidentally get your knees busted with a baseball bat."

"There's very little street crime in Murphysville." He heard the small click of the phone in the kitchen.

The extended finger pressed Lyon against the wall. "You aren't listening, pal. E. feels that a crime wave could happen to you. You might fall off that wall out there and break a leg in three, four places. If you never done that, let me tell you, you stay in the little white room for six, seven months."

"Are you threatening me?"

"Jesus! You mentally retarded or something?"

Lyon pushed the offending finger away from his chest. "You go straight to hell! Get the hell out of my house!"

"Your choice, buddy. Makes no difference to me—the easy way, a nice trip; or the hard way, a trip to the hospital."

"Get out of here!" Lyon grabbed for the man's shoulder and was surprised when it became immobile, and then his face was being pressed against the wall and his arm shoved up his back. He involuntarily groaned as his head was pressed hard against the plaster.

"The plane leaves at six tonight, buddy boy. You be on it, or by six tomorrow you won't be walking around on those pins. Understand?"

Lyon's arm was yanked further up his back until the excruciating pain made his knees buckle. He sagged toward the floor.

"LET HIM GO!" Bea stood at the base of the hallway with a meat cleaver raised over her head. "YOU HEARD ME!"

"Don't threaten, little lady." The man took three strides toward Bea, parried the cleaver blow and twisted the implement from her hands. It clattered to the floor. His hand lashed out and struck her across the face, knocking her back against the wall.

Lyon staggered to his feet and lunged. His body was knocked sideways, and he fell to the floor as an open palm came crashing against the base of his neck.

"Games are over," the quiet voice said from the doorway.

The man whirled to face Rocco. "You want some, big bastard?"

"Try me."

The two men met at the middle of the hall. Rocco's turn at the last moment threw the other man off balance. The chief's rapid chops hit under the other man's neck and across the larynx as his foot crashed on the goon's instep. As his opponent fell, Rocco's knee came up into the solar plexus. He knelt next to the gasping man, twisted his arms back and cuffed them.

Lyon struggled onto all fours and shook his head. He saw a frightened Bea by the hall door and staggered to his feet. He lurched toward her. "Are you all right?"

She put a hand to her cheek, where a red welt was beginning to appear. "Yes, I'm O.K., but you look a little glassy-eyed."

"Our friend is carrying a piece," Rocco said as he

drew a .32 from the prone man's shoulder holster.

"I got a license. A legal right to carry it."

"Let's see it." Rocco undid the cuffs and propped him against the wall. "Take it out of your wallet, nice and easy."

"I'm a licensed private investigator and have a gun permit."

"You *were* a licensed investigator," Bea said. "The secretary of the state just this minute revoked your license."

"Here's my permit." He handed Rocco a card from his wallet. Rocco glanced at it and handed it to Lyon.

Lyon looked at the name Gabriel Respampte on the permit and wondered if Gabriel had an interest in Far Eastern culture. He handed the card to Bea.

Bea glanced at the permit and ran a tentative finger across the red slash on her cheek; then she took a step into the hall lavatory and flushed the toilet. "He *had* a permit."

Rocco took the pad from his pocket. "Carrying a gun without a permit."

"Hey, wait a minute!"

"Driver's license and registration."

Mumbling, the man handed Rocco two cards. "All in order."

Rocco continued writing in his pad and, without looking at the documents, handed them to Lyon, who gave them to Bea, who flushed the toilet. "Driving without an operator's license, improper registration."

"You can't hold me on those charges!"

Rocco continued writing. "Attempted murder, two counts; extortion, two counts; carrying a concealed weapon; counts of assault, battery, disturbing the peace, resisting arrest, trespass, mischievous mischief. . . ."

"Knock it off, pig. My lawyer will get me out in two hours."

"As soon as bail is posted."

"Isn't Judge MacElroy deep-sea fishing today?" Lyon asked.

"In Florida," Rocco replied, and kept writing. He put the pad away and, bunching the man's shirt front, lifted him to his feet. "How were Esposito and Giles involved?"

"I don't know what you're talking about."

Rocco cuffed the man's hands and propelled him out the front door. There was a short scuffle outside, and Rocco reappeared at the door. "Do you have some water?"

Bea filled a bucket in the kitchen sink and handed it to Rocco. They heard the splash of water as it was thrown over the fallen man, then another crash. Rocco again appeared in the doorway. "Gabriel is terribly clumsy. Could I have some more water?"

"Wait a minute, Rocco," Lyon said. "Enough is . . ."

Rocco shrugged. "There are two other partners in the tontine. Giles, Esposito, and two others. That's all he knows, but I'm putting my money on Esposito."

8

Lyon parked the Datsun down the street from the school crossing. As if by mutual agreement, the children appeared along the walk and moved toward the patiently waiting Rocco, positioned in the center of the street. The little girls moved in small, serious clusters, while the boys hung back, engaged in the conspiratorial formation of secret clubs that would engulf them for the summer. Rocco raised his hands to stop traffic. As they moved across the street, some of the boys took furtive glances up at the towering police officer with the revolver strapped to his hip.

There was a low tap on the car window, and Lyon turned to look into a wooden salad bowl that was thrust under his nose. Several coins and two rumpled bills lay in the hollow of the bowl. He looked up at the two white-robed figures with begging bowls, standing obsequiously by the car.

"For the Kingdom of the Blossom, sir. A contribution

assures you of a place by His right hand."

Although an exact determination was difficult because of their robes and the fact that the man had had his head shaved and the girl was turbaned, he placed them at about Robin's age. "I'm afraid I don't contribute to just any guruism," Lyon said and smiled at his witticism.

The robed figures bowed politely and began to flow down the street. He wondered what lack of love, what Weltschmerz or inadequacy had bent them toward their Kingdom of the Blossom . . . which made him think of Robin—which he didn't want to do.

When the last child, small legs pumping rapidly, ran for the school, Rocco walked toward Lyon.

"I didn't know the town's police chief doubled as a school-crossing guard."

"Last day of school, and Hinton's on vacation. Meet me at the station for coffee."

The Murphysville town hall, off the green, included the selectman's office, the town clerk, library, police station and health inspector's office. The police station was on the ground floor, in front of the library. Lyon entered the small suite, waved at the dispatcher, and went into Rocco's office to start the coffee maker.

He'd made two cups and had his feet on the desk when Rocco arrived. "Well?" he asked as his friend gratefully drank the coffee.

"Nothing new. Norbert's kept me advised on the investigation."

"My visitor Gabriel?"

"We were able to set bail at fifty thousand, but he still got out. I don't know that I can make his connection with Esposito stick, either. Once his lawyer arrived, he wouldn't say a word."

"What did the state people say when we established that there had been a phone call from the lake house?"

"Norbie feels that Karen knocked her husband off at the cottage and then called her boyfriend to come out and help her get rid of the body."

"It didn't happen that way."

"Because you got a call from Giles?"

"Not just that. Whoever killed Giles tried to establish a false lead with the Carol Dodgson identification."

"Karen Giles, the pilot, or Esposito could have done that."

"Bea pointed out that there were cosmetics in the handbag along with the ID, but no mirror. Karen Giles wouldn't have made that mistake."

"But a man would have?"

"Yes."

"Well, the way it sits now, Norbert leans toward the Giles woman, and I'd put my money on Esposito or his hired gun. But where in hell do we go from here?"

Lyon brushed a forelock back from his brow. "Let me think about it, and maybe I'll have something when I see you tonight."

"Tonight?"

"We're having people in for cocktails and barbecue."

"I hope you have a lead by then, Lyon. This damn thing is playing havoc with my quota of speeding tickets."

"And also my dolphins, Rocco."

Lyon ritualistically sat at his desk before the typewriter and glanced into the machine to see whether there was an adequate amount of ribbon on the carbon spool. He adjusted the yellow second sheets on his right and the unfinished manuscript of Danny on his left. A glass of ice water sat on the far edge of the desk. He had found over the years that this almost sacramental preparation aided him in breaking out of mundane trains of thought and involved him almost immediately in what some called the "magic circle of writing."

He glanced out the window as a transient thought teased his consciousness. Robin sat on the patio with a sketch pad on her bare knees and her head tilted back to catch the sun.

It wouldn't have been quite so disconcerting if she hadn't been wearing the damn bikini. The dolphin of wise thought retreated deep into the inner recesses of his mind.

He walked slowly out onto the warm flagstones and kicked off his sneakers. She looked up and smiled. "Hi."

"We thought you'd be gone for days checking out the airports."

"Like you guys say, negative all the way."

"Forty airports in half a day or so?"

"Twenty-three in the circle you drew. This swell guy out at the Murphysville airport did it for me. I went out there first, and when he found out what I wanted, he radioed around and saved me that long trip."

"Did he take you to his A-frame for ground-school lessons?"

"Yes; how did you know? He had me on the couch when the police came and took him away."

"Robin, that was Gary Middleton. He is a suspect in this case and not the person to ask for help in tracking down a possible lead."

"Well, no one told me he was the one."

He looked down at her drawings. "And besides, your dolphins look more like fish."

She tore out the page and wadded it up. "I know. Truth of the matter is, I've never seen a dolphin."

"I've got a set of *Britannicas* in the study."

She let the sketch pad fall from her lap. "I don't believe that real things can be learned from books." She looked into his eyes. "I was thinking it might be more helpful if we rented a cabin cruiser and went out to sea."

"I wouldn't know where to look for a school of dolphins," he said hastily.

"We could try. Even if it took three or four days, and I know Bea has a lot to do at the state capital."

"Robin, no girl, even from the mountains of North Carolina, is that naïve."

"What do you mean?"

"Let me explain."

Bea Wentworth stepped from the shower, wrapped a large bath towel around herself, and went humming into the bedroom. She slowly began to dress, savoring the anticipation of tonight's party. She donned a light red pants suit. They'd use the long outdoor barbecue and serve corn on the cob smothered in butter and wrapped in foil, quartered chicken with barbecue sauce, and of course the ritual steak for the conservatives. She mentally ran over the contents of the liquor cabinet and found them adequate.

They were sitting below her window. Lyon held both Robin's hands as he leaned forward to talk intently to the young girl.

She watched them silently for a few moments, her eyes clouded. Then she stepped backward to sit heavily on the edge of the bed.

There was a knock at the door, and Kim stuck her head inside. "I have the chicken. You pick up the steaks and salad?"

Bea nodded. "In the refrigerator," she said absently.

"Are you all right?"

Bea pointed to the window. Kim strode across the room and stood looking down at the patio. She finally turned to Bea. "You want me get ma' razor and cut on her?"

"Knock it off, Kim."

"You trust him, don't you?"

"I trust Lyon implicity. . . . But I'm not sure for how long."

"Then send her home—that is, unless you plan to adopt her."

"I've tried. It's hard to keep her on airplanes."

"You know the trouble with you middle-class whiteys? You're so damn polite that you forget where things are at. Come right out and say it, for God's sake. Use a little ghetto language on the little bitch. Tell her to get her little ass back where it belongs."

"That sums it up nicely."

"You want me to lay it on her?"

Bea looked up and blinked back a tear. "Would you mind terribly?"

Bea stood at the sink, shucking corn and wrapping it in aluminum foil, as Lyon entered the kitchen. "What in hell is up with Kim?"

"A message for Garcia."

"She stormed out, and for a moment I thought she was going to push me off the parapet."

"She's delivering a message for me."

Lyon pointed an ear of corn at his wife. "You sicked her on Robin."

"Exactly."

"I was getting things in hand."

"That's what I was afraid of."

They watched Kim shake a finger under Robin's nose. Robin, with downcast eyes, talked in an inaudible whisper. Kim's hands went to the girl's shoulders.

"Robin is from the South; you don't suppose . . ." Bea said in a soft voice.

"Better than South Boston. But Christ only knows what Kim will say when she gets going."

As they watched, the two women fell into each other's arms. Robin buried her head in Kim's shoulder, and then broke away and ran for the house. The kitchen door banged open. Robin stopped and stared at Bea and Lyon a moment, broke into a sob, and ran for the stairs.

Kim entered the kitchen slowly and stood by the doorway.

"What did you say to her?" Lyon asked.

"I told her to get the hell back home, and then she . . ." Tears coursed over Kim's cheeks. "And then she told me how it felt, how much it meant to her, what it was . . . it was a lovely, sweet, innocent and beautiful thing. . . ." Kim choked and ran from the room.

"I don't think the ghetto makes them as tough these days," Bea said and handed Lyon thirty-two ears of corn to husk.

The lieutenant governor stood in the center of the patio beneath the gently swaying lanterns and brought his hand down in a long chopping motion. ". . . and then she said, 'Today we unlock the pay toilets, and tomorrow the world.'"

There was laughter from the surrounding group as Lyon moved away from the periphery of the crowd toward the long barbecue at the far end of the patio. Rocco Herbert, looking slightly ridiculous in a high chef's hat, brought a large steak impaled on the end of a fork over to the barbecue and delicately dropped it onto the coals. He looked up at Lyon. "How'd I get snookered into this?" he asked as he flipped over the steak.

"I think your wife volunteered you," Lyon said, "and unless you're feeding a lion, you had better flip that steak back again."

"How about another drink?"

"I'm psychic," Lyon said and handed his friend a double vodka.

"Does being a great raconteur help in politics?" Rocco gestured with the long fork toward the lieutenant governor.

"About as much as money, which is to say a lot."

"What about Bea?"

"She's one of the few with causes."

"Have you come up with any ideas on the Giles killing?"

"I've tried to work on it, but things have been diverting around here today."

Rocco glanced toward the kitchen door, where Robin, dressed in a misty blue dress cut deep at the neckline, was talking with Damon Snow. "I hope they weren't *too* diverting."

"Speaking of Miss Diverting, she checked out the airports with Gary Middleton."

"Oh, God!"

"Can you recheck?"

"I'll put some men on it tomorrow morning. With school closed we have more manpower."

Lyon felt a hand on his shoulder and turned to face Snow. The toy manufacturer's eyes were slightly out of focus, and he walked and talked with the great care and articulation of the nearly drunk. "I believe your friend the lieutenant governor is dominating the party, and that he is bombastic, and how am I going to make out with the chick?"

Lyon frowned and looked toward Robin. "Make out?"

Damon blinked. "She's a lovely young lady, and I wish to learn her views on many topics."

The heavy voice of the lieutenant governor boomed over the patio. "Now, I'm not saying who this certain U.S. senator is, but his brother was president." There was appreciative knowing laughter from the group surrounding him.

Damon Snow stood solemnly erect. "He is now

maligning a U.S. senator from an honored family."

"It's just an anecdote," Lyon said.

"The Walking Wobblies," Damon replied with a raised finger.

"What?"

"Wait and see." Damon hurried toward the house.

"He's getting a snootful," Rocco said.

"He was the first to arrive and insisted on a double for openers."

Kim snatched the fork from Rocco's hand and quickly turned the steak. "The rest of us don't like them burned, and when are you going to bust those jokers wandering around town in the white robes?"

"The Blossom people?"

"I don't know what they call themselves," the black woman replied, "but anybody in white robes is on my list."

"They're a perfectly harmless religious group."

"Didn't they buy the old Claxton mansion on Plank Road?" Lyon asked.

"Right. I went out there and checked them over. Bunch of religious nuts, mostly kids, who believe that Doctor Blossom is the reincarnation of John the Baptist or something. They have a school bus, and every morning they truck the kids around the state to panhandle."

"If they were black you'd have the health inspector and building inspector close the place down," Kim said, and flipped the steak onto a platter.

Rocco sighed. "If they were black, Kim, we'd have a baseball party."

"What's that?"

"Twenty-two guys with baseball bats do a number on them."

"You go . . ."

They turned in unison at the whirring sound of a tick-tick. Damon was taking three-foot-high Wobbly dolls from a large box. When he threw a small lever in each doll's back, it began a slow march toward the lieutenant governor, who was holding forth at the center of the patio. Damon had also inserted a fork in the paw of each Wobbly. He started the last of the six dolls and stood to watch them proceed toward the unsuspecting politician.

"Sic 'em," he said, lurched, and grabbed the door to steady himself.

They sat in the study with drinks in their hands and stared soberly at the blackboard filled with Lyon's clumsy printing. "I could sum the whole case up in one word," Rocco said and pulled at his vodka.

"Exactly," Lyon responded.

Outside the room, swirling through the study window, the party din rose and fell in tidelike waves. The two men were quiet, each mulling over the death of Giles: Rocco in a pragmatic proceeding manner, from one plateau to another; Lyon through a haze of memories. Now and then an individual voice or laugh would isolate itself temporarily from the party group on the patio, and Lyon seemed to hear Tom Giles from a year before.

"You know, Went, someday I'm going to mount a machine gun on that crate of mine and shoot you out of the sky. You're a menace."

"I don't buzz people's homes at six on a Sunday morning like some I could name."

"You couldn't buzz a Christmas tree. And to think I once thought there was hope for you. That's what comes from being friends with a Townie."

"Townie? Good God, Tom. I'd almost forgotten the word." But he hadn't. "I sometimes think you're sorry you ever had to leave Greenfield."

Tom had stood at the edge of the patio, looked down

at the river, and spoken quietly. "I think maybe I am.
Funny how those days seem more real to me than the true world. Everything went right then—everything worked; now, everything seems like the White Rabbit, always late for a very important date." He had turned and the spell was broken. "What the hell? Hey, you know, we don't see each other enough these days. Have to correct that."

They hadn't, and now Tom was dead and the debt still outstanding. An old debt of pubescent gratitude—perhaps the most important kind. Lyon sighed.

"You've got something."

"No. I was just wondering how you felt when you beat up Gabriel What's-his-name."

"Ring in the Civil Liberties Union," the big man muttered sullenly into his drink.

"I'm grateful that you saved us from a sojourn in the hospital. It's just that you're paradoxical. That morning I saw you directing small kids across the street, and I saw how you looked at them. That doesn't fit in with my trespassing visitor getting the hose treatment in the driveway."

Rocco shrugged. "I still feel for the kids, but somewhere along the line they become teenagers, hop cars, take drugs, break into the A & P. Maybe that's why I want to get out of this work. It brutalizes you. It can't help it, even in a small town like this. God only knows what it does to you in a large city, where you face the crap every shift."

A girl's scream carried to them from the patio. Rocco stood up instinctively.

"Take it easy," Lyon said. "Probably nothing but fun and games."

"NOT HARDLY," Bea said from the doorway. "Damon is attacking Robin."

"What's wrong with him tonight?"

"He's zonked," Bea said and placed a restraining hand on Lyon. "No knights. Let Rocco handle it."

Robin stood wild-eyed in the corner of the patio, her bodice ripped down one shoulder, as Damon held to the parapet with both hands and leered at her. "He wanted to see the barn," Robin said, "and then he . . ."

"Come on, Damon." Rocco put an arm around Damon's shoulders and led him firmly toward the house. The party voices, which had stilled for a moment, rose to their former level.

Once inside the kitchen, Damon broke away from Rocco, swiveled across the floor, and fell heavily against the sink. "You didn't have to shove."

"How about some coffee?"

"Screw the coffee. Gimme a drink."

Bea silently poured a large mug of black coffee and placed it on the counter next to Damon. "You'll feel better," she said.

"Another drink and I'll be all right."

"How much has he had?" Rocco asked in an aside to Lyon.

"He had a snootful an hour ago, and God only knows how much since."

"A drink!" Damon demanded.

"No," Bea said firmly. "Coffee and something to eat."

Damon groaned. "You want to make me sick?"

"I want to make you sober."

"All right, if that's the way it is." He pulled himself erect and carefully planted his feet apart. He stared at them with dull eyes, his face slack. "I can take a hint. No booze here. I'll go to a bar." He peered intently toward the door as if sighting a course, and then began to move laboriously across the room.

Rocco caught his arm. "Give me the keys, Damon."

"Take your hands off me. I am perfectly capable of driving a car."

"Nope. The keys."

Damon shoved Rocco's hands away and backed against the wall. "Try and get them, big boy."

With resignation, Rocco looked over at Lyon and then stepped resolutely toward Damon, who now held his arms defensively in front of him. As Rocco stepped closer, Damon's fist lashed out. It was caught in Rocco's hand and bent behind his own back.

"Right-hand trouser pocket," Lyon said.

"Right." Rocco flipped the keys from the pinned man's pocket to Lyon, who tossed them to Bea, who tossed them inside the refrigerator freezer.

"My lawyers will hear about this in the morning," Damon said to the wall.

"In the morning you won't remember a thing," Rocco replied.

"He can sleep on the couch tonight," Bea said.

"I want to sleep in the barn with your guest," Damon mumbled as he spied a liquor bottle on the drainboard and lunged for it.

"You'll love the windjammer cruise. Kids your own age, the open sea, the chance to study dolphins firsthand. A marvelous opportunity. The boat leaves from New London this afternoon, and do you want me to help you pack your things?" Bea sat back against the breakfast-nook bench and smiled across the table at Robin.

Lyon stood near the sink and looked out over the distant river below. The morning sun hurt his eyes, and he poured a steaming mug of coffee from the percolator and waited for Robin's reply.

"My dolphin drawings don't look so hot," Robin said, "but I thought Lyon and I could . . ."

"Lyon couldn't possibly get away. He's up to his ears in the Giles murder case."

"I could help," Robin said hopefully.

"Asking a suspect in the case to help check out a missing airplane isn't much help, dear."

"Gary seemed to be so nice."

"Where's our other house guest?" Lyon asked.

Bea motioned toward the living room. "He's locked in."

Lyon unlocked the door and stepped into the living room. The room was rank with the smell of liquor, stale cigarette smoke, and drunken male. Damon Snow lay on the couch, one arm extended across his eyes, the other outstretched as if reaching for the empty liquor bottle lying on its side in front of the couch.

"You awake?" Lyon asked softly.

"Don't shout. Let me die peacefully."

"Do you remember last night?"

There was a long pause from the prone man and then the arm was slowly removed from his eyes as he sat up to stare at Lyon. "My God! Can you and Bea ever forgive me? I don't know what got into me."

"About a quart or so, I'd judge."

"That girl. The one I went into the barn with and . . ."

"She's in the kitchen."

"What will I say to her? And to Bea and Rocco? Oh, Christ! That isn't like me, Lyon."

"It can happen to anyone, with too much liquor."

"Rocco's on the phone," Bea called from the kitchen.

"He probably wants to arrest me," Damon said and put his hands to his head.

Lyon smiled and picked up the extension phone. "Damon wants to know what charges you have against him," he said into the receiver.

"Being a damn fool," Rocco replied. "Norbert just called."

"A break in the case?"

"Not quite. Esposito's dead."

9

The door to the house on Braeland Drive was opened by a uniformed officer before Lyon and Rocco were midway up the walk. Lyon glanced down at the empty shoe rack in the vestibule, shrugged, and followed Rocco through the house toward the indoor swimming pool.

The fully clothed body of the fat man lay beside the pool. The police photographer had taken the low table from the *shoin* and stood on it to obtain a full-length picture of the corpse. Captain Norbert, huddled with his corporals, frowned at Lyon as they crossed toward him.

"What's the story?" Rocco asked.

Norbert looked toward one of the corporals, who immediately snapped open a small pad and began to read: "At 0805 a call was received at the barracks from an individual identifying himself as Mr. Koyota, a household employee of the deceased. Mr. Koyota stated that he reported for work at his usual time and discovered the deceased face-down in the pool. Troopers Willcox and Storey arrived on the scene at 0824, made a preliminary examination of the deceased, and placed a call to the medical examiner's office."

"Where's the doc?"

"Contemplating his navel over behind the diving board," Norbert replied.

In the far corner, a small man in rumpled seersucker was staring into the pool. "I could have one of these if I were in private practice," he said as Lyon and Rocco approached.

"What can you tell us, Doc?" Rocco asked.

"I'd estimate a pool like this, with the solarium roof, could cost as much as . . ."

"About the deceased?"

"Oh, him. A massive cranial blow, with water in the lungs. Exact time of death and cause unknown until the autopsy."

"Hit on the head and thrown in the water?"

"Possibly. I'll narrow it down in my final report."

Rocco turned back to Captain Norbert. "How do you see it, Norbie?"

"Two probables. Esposito surprised a burglary in progress, there was a struggle; he was hit on the head and either was thrown or fell into the pool. Second, we all know about Esposito's syndicate connections . . . for political reasons the powers that be felt he should be removed."

"A contract?"

"We're not discounting it."

"There are some valuable works of art here," Lyon said. "Have they been checked out?"

"The houseboy is taking inventory now."

"He wasn't killed in the house," Lyon said.

"And how in hell do you come up with that?" the

trooper captain asked, turning a light shade of red.

"He's got his shoes on."

"So?"

"He would have taken them off automatically in the outside vestibule."

"I think he's right," Rocco agreed.

"Don't just stand there!" Norbert yelled at the two corporals. "Check around the house."

As if propelled by a released spring, the two troopers moved quickly from the room. In a few moments, Lyon could see one of them walking heavily through the *hira-niwa,* kicking the smoothed ruffles of sand. He cringed. "What does Koyota say?"

Norbert looked puzzled. "Who?"

"Esposito's butler-houseman."

"Like the report said, he called us when he found the body. Last night he prepared and served dinner, then left for the night, and didn't return until eight this morning."

"I'd like to talk to him," Lyon said.

They found the Japanese houseman in a front room, with an insurance list attached to a clipboard. He moved slowly through the room, checking items against the list. He bowed silently as Rocco and Lyon entered, then cast a rueful look at their shod feet.

"Anything missing?" Rocco asked.

"It would seem not. I have one more room to inventory, but the more valuable pieces have been accounted for."

"We just found six hundred bucks in the deceased's wallet," Norbert said from the doorway. "Robbery's out."

"Would you please describe all your activities yesterday?" Lyon asked.

"I cleaned house in the morning, dusted, waxed, and paid special attention to the garden and pool. Mr.

 Esposito was very particular about the pool and insisted that no additives be placed in the water, so it must continually be cleaned thoroughly. I spent most of yesterday afternoon scrubbing the pool. When Mr. Esposito arrived home at six, I prepared and served dinner. I left before seven."

"The medical examiner will want the exact contents of the meal you served."

"It was one of his favorites. He had it at least once a week."

"Which was?"

"*Gohan, osuimono, sashimi, tempura, tsukemono* and *chawan mushi.*"

"That's a hell of a big help," Captain Norbert said from the doorway.

"Translate, please."

"Rice, soup, raw fish, shrimp in batter, pickled vegetables and custard."

"What about your whereabouts last night, Koyota?"

The diminutive Japanese bowed with a slight smile. "I believe there is an American saying—was getting ashes hauled."

"Laid?"

"The two ladies of the night will testify if necessary."

"Two?" Rocco asked incredulously.

"Their other friend was indisposed."

Perspiration beaded Sarge's forehead as he wrestled the beer keg under the bar, tapped it, and ran foam from the spigot until he'd bled it properly.

"Do you have any Dry Sack under there?" Lyon asked.

"You bet." A bottle was plunked on the bar, and a glass slid along the polished surface. "Where's the chief?"

"He'll be along."

"Ever tell you about the time we were pinned down near Inchon, and the chief—he was a captain then—held a mortar with his bare hands and . . ."

Lyon had heard the story several times and knew he'd hear it again. He tried to concentrate through Sarge's tale of charging Chinese and Rocco's courage. Esposito had been involved with Giles, and the two dead men had been involved with two others in the tontine. If Esposito was involved, there had to be a great deal of money in the situation. Since Giles was involved, the situation required legal expertise. But who were the others?

"Got a dollar's worth of change, Sarge?"

"Hey, you usually ask for a dime."

"This call's to Hartford."

Sarge rang the register and flipped the quarters to Lyon. "Know how much change you've borrowed over the years?"

"I'll settle up next time I come in," Lyon said as he dialed the state capital from the wall phone.

"I put her on the windjammer cruise and waved bye-bye until it was out of sight," Bea said when she picked up on her extension. "No way she can get off without swimming through shark-infested waters."

"I need you to run a check on a corporation for me, hon . . ."

"Sure. What's the name?"

"I don't know."

"It's harder that way, Lyon," Bea said with a trace of sarcasm.

"Esposito and Giles were probably two of the officers, and I'd like to know the names of the other officers and major stockholders."

"Lyon, this office has over forty-three thousand domestic corporations registered, not including churches and foreign corporations."

"I thought that if you looked through the forms and

 picked out the one that had both Esposito's and Giles's names . . ."

"You're stark raving mad! We'd have to examine each and every file!"

"Thanks, Bea. 'Preciate it. And listen, don't run them all, just corporations chartered in the last year or two."

Rocco entered the bar slowly and gingerly slid onto the stool next to Lyon. A drink was wordlessly poured for him. Sarge and Lyon watched the police officer gulp it down.

"You look awful."

Rocco signaled for another drink. "Do you know that in all my years of police work and military service, I thought I had seen everything? I've seen traffic accidents where we had to pry the bodies up with crowbars, and I've watched artillery landing in some poor guy's foxhole . . . but I had never been to an autopsy before. Do you know what the doctor does? He takes a knife and . . ."

"Never mind," Lyon interrupted. "The results will be sufficient."

"Death by drowning. A massive blow to the head rendered him unconscious, but he drowned in the pool."

"Time of death?"

"He could fix it pretty definitely because of the progression of the rather distinctive food remnants in the digestive tract and the knowledge of exactly when he ate."

"And?"

"Midnight. Give or take a few minutes either way."

"He's sure of that?"

"Said he'd testify to it in court."

Bea Wentworth put her hands on Kim's shoulders and stooped to peer over her deputy's shoulder into the microfilm reader. Pages blurred past until Kim stopped the wheel's movement and adjusted the focus.

"We came up with twenty other corporations with Giles named as an officer, but this is the only one that lists both him and Esposito," Kim said.

"As a lawyer, he would often appear as an incorporator for his clients, but this is the one we want. Can you have a print made and bring it to my office?"

"Give me five minutes."

Bea was lost in thought as she sat behind her desk. She made notes on a legal pad. The Darling Corporation's major listed activity was buying and selling real estate. She listed the four corporate officers. The notes trailed off into a scrawl that changed to doodles. Bea found that she had formed the outline of an airplane. She reached for the phone.

"Get me the director of the FAA in Washington," she told her secretary. "The Federal Aviation Agency. Wait a minute—a deputy director will do, someone who handles the issuance of pilot's licenses."

While Bea was talking to Washington, Kim entered and placed the print-out from the microfilm on her desk. Her eyebrows rose as Bea finished the call. "Well?"

Bea looked off into space, and then picked up the print-out. She studied it for a few minutes.

"Well?" Kim asked again.

"I think we have another job cut out for us."

"What this time?"

Bea tapped the print-out. "The company was chartered just after the first of the year and lists its primary activity as real estate."

"I see, said the blind man. You want to know what real estate they're fooling around with."

"You know, Kim, you're bright."

"I'm not bright enough to know how to do it. There's nothing in our records that will disclose real-estate transactions for any company, much less this Darling Corporation."

"The town clerks will know."

"Not another one hundred and sixty-nine calls?"

"Yep. Now, deeds in this state are filed by individual towns, and each town clerk can run the indices to find out whether any property has been conveyed to the Darling Corporation since its inception."

"Come on, Beatrice. You know how some of those town clerks are: they're ancient, don't work very hard, and won't give you the time of day if they have to turn their heads to see the clock."

"Tell them the request is from the governor."

"You can be impeached, you know."

"I know. And then we'd go back to the state Senate, where we belong."

"I always enjoy a ride in the country," Lyon said, "but will you please tell me where we're going?"

"NOPE!"

"You're looking as smug as the time you blocked MacKay from the gubernatorial nomination. The cat who ate the chicken sort of look."

"THAT'S CANARY, WENTWORTH!"

"Whatever. You must have consumed the whole damn coop."

"CAGE!"

"How come those hearing aids never seem to work right?"

"What?"

"Never mind."

The gently rolling Connecticut countryside sharpened as the road approached the Berkshire foothills in the northwest quadrant of the state. A gentle breeze sparked green hues off dense foliage as the road wound toward a small valley.

Lyon turned to Bea as she stopped in front of the village's town hall. "Penobscot? I never would have thought you had many supporters here."

"They are a little reactionary," Bea said as they walked up the steps. "In fact, last November, I think there were twenty write-in votes for King George III. I want to show you something on the land records."

The town clerk's office, located at the rear of the building, consisted of a small front room with two desks and a large vault containing numerous heavy volumes of deeds and mortgages. A dour white-haired woman in her early sixties looked up from a ledger with a frown.

Bea smiled broadly and stepped forward to shake hands. "How good to see you again, Mrs. Wainwright."

The clerk ignored Bea's hand. "Welfare chiselers should be hanged."

"We were going to hang two or three hundred of them, but you know how the Supreme Court is."

"Ought to hang them, too."

Bea's smile remained transfixed. "I hope it's all right for the loyal opposition to look at a book or two in the vault?"

"They're public records."

Lyon looked apprehensively at the heavy vault door as they stepped inside. "You don't suppose she'll lock us in, do you?" he whispered to Bea.

"There's always that possibility," Bea replied. She ran a finger over several ledgers until she found the one she wanted. She lugged it to a high table and began to thumb through the pages of documents.

"Will you please tell me what's going on?"

"I'll have it in a minute. In the meanwhile, read this." She handed Lyon the microfilm print-out of the Darling Corporation's charter.

While Lyon read the document, Bea pulled out two more volumes of land records and located the additional pages.

"Good God," Lyon said softly.

"It's the only charter we could locate that had both Giles's and Esposito's names on it."

"And the two others. It's hard to believe."

"It doesn't necessarily prove anything."

Lyon leaned against the vault wall, holding the document limply in one hand. "Toranga Blossom."

"What did Rocco tell you about the Most Reverend Dr. Blossom? That he's the reincarnation of John the Baptist or something?"

"And Damon Snow's name." Lyon thought over his relationship with the toy manufacturer for a moment. "Well, we know it's not Damon."

"How's that?"

"Damon was at our house the night Esposito was killed. If you'll remember, at the exact time of the killing, midnight, he was drunk and attacking Robin."

"And we were all with him when the plane went down."

"But the Reverend Dr. Blossom . . . that's another question. What else do you have?"

"We ran the charter for the Darling Corporation, found four names listed, and their major activity described as real property."

"And now you've discovered that Darling has property here in Penobscot."

"Right." Bea pointed to the first volume on the table. "In April the Darling Corporation purchased a large tract of land for eight hundred thousand dollars. On the same day they took out a land loan in the amount of four hundred thousand dollars."

"Mr. E. mentioned a tontine. I can't figure out how that fits into a perfectly legal land purchase."

"Four weeks later the Darling Corporation conveyed the same property to four individuals as joint tenants."

Lyon looked at the deed. "Conveyed to Giles,

Esposito, Blossom and Damon Snow. The tontine."

"How's that?"

"I'll explain later. Right now, I'd like to look at that property."

Using the property description from the deed and the large topographical map in the clerk's office, they were able to pinpoint the location of the acreage as being near the Interstate highway, several miles from the village center.

They parked on the grassy shoulder, with the car's wheels canted into a drainage ditch. Lyon held the rusty strands of barbed wire apart as Bea slipped between them and began to walk through the meadow. He bent to pick up a clump of dirt and let it run through his fingers. "Good land."

"From what you've told me of Sal Esposito, I can't imagine him turning farmer."

A high wooded hill rose at the far extreme of the property. The highway bordered the property to the south, and they could hear the distant murmur of traffic. Something bright glinted in the sun from the direction of the highway, and they walked toward the reflecting object.

As they neared the transit on its tripod, they could see the surveyor with his head at the eyepiece, signaling to the distant rod man with an upraised arm. He looked up as they approached. "Help you folks?"

"Why are you surveying here?"

The engineer folded the tripod and hefted it over his shoulder. "New highway exit ramp."

Lyon looked at Bea. "I think maybe our tontine members weren't going to grow barley after all."

Bea sighed. "I know. The state highway commissioner wants the first congressional district nomination next year and will talk with me confidentially."

"Exactly."

Kim and Bea simultaneously shuddered as the chalk squeaked. "Motive," Lyon wrote.

"WE CAN DO WITHOUT THE CHALK TALK!" Bea said and took the chalk from his fingers. "Just tell us."

"Thank God," Rocco said into his vodka. "Can we hurry up? I've got to get home before dark."

"O.K.," Lyon said. "Let me run through it. Tom Giles was one of the most prominent real-estate lawyers in the area. He also represented many other clients, including Damon Snow and his factory, Dr. Blossom, and the Dauntless Racing Company."

"Why Dr. Blossom?" Kim asked.

"Happenstance. When the doctor and his disciples came to Connecticut and bought the Claxton mansion, they retained Tom to handle the purchase and also to help them qualify as a religious corporation under the statutes."

"How do you know that?" Rocco asked.

Lyon gestured toward Bea. "The charter at the secretary of state's office shows that Blossom's papers were filed by Giles, and the land records in Murphysville indicate that the deed to the Blossom people was returned to Giles as attorney of record."

"I'm with you," Rocco said. "That establishes the initial relationship between Giles and Dr. Blossom. How does Damon Snow fit in?"

"Tom represented Damon for years."

"And Esposito?"

"We can only conjecture about that. As I see it, Tom Giles knew that the racing company was looking for a large tract of land in a town that would be receptive to the track. He also knew of such a parcel, but couldn't swing the purchase cash by himself. He persuaded Damon to put in a share, and then Dr. Blossom, because he knew that the religious group was heavily into real estate. I think he approached Esposito when he couldn't raise the rest of the cash and began to get desperate."

"Right, so they all climbed into bed together."

"Giles formed the Darling Corporation, purchased the land, and optioned it to the racing company immediately after they had conveyed the land to themselves as joint tenants."

"Do you know the option price?"

"Friends at the State Gaming Commission were helpful," Bea said. "The option will be exercised next month at five million dollars."

"My God!"

Kim looked puzzled. "I still don't see which or what is a tontine."

"The land is now held in the name of the four individuals as joint tenants."

Rocco pulled on his drink and rattled ice. "My wife and I own our house in survivorship. Is that the same?"

"Not exactly," Lyon said. "As joint tenants, on the death of one, the property automatically passes to the remaining owners without passing through the estate of the deceased."

"Ah. The last man in gets the whole pie."

"For a cash investment of a hundred thousand dollars, the survivor of the tontine will make five million."

"Then it's Damon or Dr. Blossom."

"All of us here are witnesses to Damon Snow's whereabouts the night Esposito was killed."

"Wait a minute," Kim said excitedly. "The Giles plane held only two people, right? So if either Snow or Blossom is a pilot, we've got him, right?"

"Wrong," Bea retorted. "I checked with the FAA. Neither of them is or ever has been a licensed pilot."

"They could have paid someone."

"They could have."

The phone rang, and as Lyon automatically reached for it, Rocco put his fingers to his lips. "If it's Helen, I left five minutes ago."

"Yes," Lyon said into the receiver, and then he passed it to Rocco.

Rocco looked stricken. "I told you: five minutes ago," he whispered, with his hand over the mouthpiece. "Yes, Chief Herbert here. . . . When, Norbie? . . . Are you sure? . . . Thanks. Be down in the morning." He hung up and stood. "That's it."

"Not another . . ."

"No. The State Police have just arrested Karen Giles and Gary Middleton for the murder of Tom Giles."

"There's not enough evidence for a conviction," Lyon said.

"There is now. They obtained a search warrant and went into Middleton's A-frame. The murder weapon was found hidden in the springs of the couch. Ballistics positively identifies it as the weapon that killed Giles."

10

The Cedarcrest Toy Company was housed in a low modernistic building that nestled in the woods on the outskirts of town. Rocco turned the cruiser through the covered bridge spanning the narrow Morgan River. Beyond the river, a broad, flat field stretched toward the woods and the secluded parking lot of the factory. As they walked toward the executive offices, Lyon stopped before a rustic sign:

CEDARCREST TOYS
A delight to millions

Guided Tours: Tuesdays and Thursdays 10:00 A.M.

"I should do that someday," he said, half aloud.

Rocco grabbed his arm. "Come on."

In the waiting room, Rocco approached the reception desk while Lyon stood admiringly before a glass case of handcrafted lead soldiers arranged in a duplication of the Battle of Bunker Hill.

"Damon will be with us in five minutes," Rocco said. "I think I have something."

"Damn! I knew you would. It's Dr. Blossom, right?"

"The Tarantula and the Toys."

"Christ!"

Damon Snow's office was a slanted, windowless oval. In the center of the room a draftsman's table was mounted on a swivel platform. The perimeter of the room was illuminated with pinpoint spotlights in various colors that shone on a dozen dolls, all alike, placed in various positions.

The table swiveled to face the door as Damon looked up and slid off the stool. "Lyon, Rocco, good to see you." He shook hands warmly. "I'm sober, Chief, I really am. Haven't had a drink since that ignominious night of the party."

"It can happen to anyone," Rocco said.

Lyon stooped to examine one of the dolls. Each doll, blond hair hanging to her waist, stood before a mirror frame. "Of course. It's Alice and the Looking Glass."

"That's right. They're the first run of a new line we're thinking of putting out. I like to bring them in to live with me for a week or so. That way I can make necessary changes—turn the mouth perhaps, a larger smile, whatever. Last week I had a dozen six-foot Wobblies living with me. Crowded as hell."

Rocco and Lyon sat in Swedish side chairs as Damon leaned against the drawing board. "You didn't tell us you were involved with Tom Giles," Rocco said abruptly.

"You didn't ask."

"That's a hell of an answer."

"That was a hell of a question. There's never been any secret about it. Tom was my attorney for ten years. He handled all our corporate legal work, purchase of this property, our trademarks, the whole works."

"And the Darling Corporation."

Damon slid onto the stool and propped his elbows on the drawing board. "That was a side business deal. Tom talked me into taking a piece of the action. Said we'd all make a bundle."

"How much?"

"You know, fellows, we're friends and all that, but don't you think my financial affairs are my own private business?"

"Not in the case of murder."

"You think Tom's death was tied to the Darling Corporation?"

"It's possible."

"I saw in this morning's paper that the police have charged Karen Giles and her boyfriend."

"That doesn't explain Esposito's death—another partner of yours."

"Hey, come on! You two aren't serious."

"Whose idea was it to transfer the property from the corporation to individuals as joint tenants?" Lyon asked.

"I'm not quite sure; it seemed to be a mutual understanding at the time. Tom told us he was in marital difficulties, and we could all envision a divorce dispute over money, and legal action that might attach his shares and not allow us to sell the parcel. Tom felt that taking the property jointly might help somewhat. Wait a minute. If the police have charged Karen Giles, how do they explain Esposito? The way the property is held, Karen doesn't get a dime out of it. She doesn't stand to benefit by either death, unless you call getting rid of her husband a benefit."

"No. Only you and Dr. Blossom benefit as far as the property is concerned."

"What about Esposito?" Damon pressed.

"The State Police mark it up as an organization hit."

"And you don't?"

"No," Lyon said quietly. "You were aware of the tontine effect of the new deed?"

"Tontine?"

"That the survivors automatically receive the deceased's portion."

"Well, yes. But it was set up to keep it away from Karen, and Tom said there would be certain tax advantages."

Lyon tented his fingers and leaned back in his chair to think over what he knew of Damon Snow. Ten years earlier he had arrived unannounced at Nutmeg Hill to plead for the rights to manufacture Wobbly dolls. During the course of the afternoon, they had struck a bargain and had notified Tom Giles to draw up the proper papers. Later he had driven Damon through Murphysville. Damon had shown an interest in the region and asked for a tour of the surrounding area.

"I've never really grown up," Damon had told him that afternoon. "Believe it or not, my father was a pickle canner, and if anything is likely to turn a person off when he considers his future life, canning pickles will do it. I kicked around a lot, dropped out of several distinguished colleges, and finally by chance landed a temporary job in the design room of a large toy company. I stayed for two years, and when Dad died and the pickle empire passed to me, I sold it off and started my own toy company."

An innocuous background, Lyon thought. A pleasant, productive life, and as far as he knew, except for the one drunken escapade, Damon was a decent person. But then, five million dollars could stretch a lot of honor.

The smile had long faded from Damon's face as he looked belligerently at Rocco. "You know, Herbert, it just occurred to me that I don't like your attitude."

"I never thought of myself as being in a popularity contest."

“The first selectman will hear of this. You can’t barge into a responsible businessman’s office and start accusing him of murder. I find your attitude particularly obnoxious since you know damn well where I was when both men were killed. I was with you—the two of you.”

“We’re making routine inquiries, Mr. Snow,” Rocco said with an undertone of veiled authority.

“You are? A small-town cop and a children’s writer who used to be my friend. . . . Leave it to the professionals.”

“Don’t get temperamental, Damon,” Lyon said.

“Crap! I’m waiting for the next question—whether I hired some hood to knock those guys off.”

“We’re not suggesting any such thing.”

“Why don’t you talk to that Oriental creep, Dr. Blossom?”

“We intend to.”

“You were in the service, weren’t you?” Lyon asked.

“Same time as you two guys. What did they call it?—World War Two Point Five.”

“Air Force?”

“Army. My branch was artillery. If you ever find anyone knocked off with a 155 howitzer, I might be your man. Now, do you mind?”

“Thank you for your cooperation,” Rocco said automatically.

“Alice in Wonderland,” Lyon said. “Through the Looking Glass.”

“What’s that supposed to mean?” Damon asked irritably.

“Nothing was as it seemed,” Lyon responded.

Rocco stopped the police cruiser inside the small covered bridge over the Morgan River. He hunched over the wheel.

“Forget something?”

"I was just thinking what a great place this would be for a speed trap. I'll put the radar unit up the road in the tall grass and . . ."

"Come on, Rocco."

"O.K." He turned the ignition key, and the car jumped out of the bridge, squealed as it turned into the right-hand lane and accelerated toward Plank Road. "Damon can be scratched as a suspect. We're his alibi."

"Accomplices?"

"Unlikely. Do you realize how difficult it really is to hire someone to kill somebody? If you're like Damon, it's almost impossible. If you're a man with Esposito's background, the going rate is about three thousand. The ordinary middle-class person just has no way of making contact with a hit man."

"Which leaves Toranga Blossom."

"The Reverend Doctor," Rocco replied and turned onto the access road toward the Claxton mansion.

The Claxton mansion was a tall white house in the Venetian style. A high wall breached only by large wrought-iron gates surrounded the property. Rocco braked the cruiser in front of the gate, with the fender brushing the metal, and honked impatiently.

"This had been the Claxton homestead for three generations," Lyon said. "I was surprised when they sold it."

"The last of the line bought a condominium in Florida. And unless he's got a crew of disciples willing to work for free, who could afford to run and maintain an elephant like this?"

A triumvirate of white-robed young men with shaved heads moved slowly down the drive toward the gates. There was open hostility in their faces as they looked toward the police car. Rocco stuck his head out the window. "Official business."

They exchanged glances, then one stepped forward. "This is sacred ground, and unless you have a warrant . . ."

"Listen, sonny. I can get a warrant. But if I do, I will be ticked off, and that bodes no good for sacred ground. Now, open the damn gate, or do I have to run this vehicle through it?"

As the gate reluctantly swung open, Rocco waited until the aperture was wide enough for the car, and then gunned down the winding drive with a screech of tires.

"You're proving something," Lyon said as they approached the portico.

"Probably. You know, I wish I could get my lawn to look like this."

"Get some disciples."

The car stopped under the arch, and they were met by two more robed figures who seemed to have been cloned from the original three. "Dr. Blossom here?"

"It is time for his morning meditation," a low voice answered.

"I'd like him to meditate with me a few minutes," Rocco said.

One of the disciples hurriedly shuffled off. Lyon and Rocco, standing on the white steps in front of the ornate front door, were closely observed by the remaining disciples. "How are the townspeople taking the establishment of this religious community?" Lyon asked.

"Badly. I'm getting it from both ends: petitions from residents and calls from irate parents who want me to raid the place and get their kids back."

"Wait until the kidnapping for deprogramming starts."

"That's one hassle I'll gladly leave to Norbie."

"Did you know that before the Mormons made the

 trek from Illinois to Utah, Nauvoo was the largest city west of Philadelphia?"

"I'll remember that," Rocco said as he glanced up at the returning disciple.

"This way, please."

They were led through the mansion to a glass-paneled door through which the Reverend Dr. Blossom could be seen bending over a white desk. The disciple knocked discreetly, and Blossom motioned them in. Lyon slipped out of his sneakers, padded to the desk and bowed. "Dr. Toranga Blossom, I am Lyon Wentworth."

The Oriental looked up. He was resplendent in white trousers, white shoes and a soft white turtleneck. He stepped around the desk with an extended hand. "Call me Tony."

Lyon, nonplused, straightened and automatically extended his hand. "We're sorry to impose on your meditation."

Blossom waved a deprecating hand. "Just a P and L on a fast-food franchise I'm thinking of getting into." He motioned toward a corner of the room where a deep white sofa and easy chairs were arranged in a semicircle. "Doesn't the hot pavement hurt your feet?"

Lyon looked at his bare feet, and then across the room to where his sneakers were neatly aligned by the door. "I think I will put them on." He slipped his feet into the sneakers and paused before a picture frame containing a mounted scarf and a white ribbon with a red spot in the center.

Blossom smiled at Rocco. "I can imagine the purpose of your visit, Chief Herbert. Mr. Wentworth has a son or daughter who has become one of my disciples, and he's requested that you intercede."

"We have another purpose."

"A scarf of a thousand threads and a *hachimaki,*" Lyon said before the picture frame.

"Ah, you recognize them, Mr. Wentworth. One of the few mementos brought from my native country."

"They are very rare," Lyon said. "I understand that most of them were destroyed with the . . ."

"With the death of the wearer. Indeed, that was usually the case."

"A relative?"

"No, mine. When I volunteered for the Divine Wind, as an officer of the Imperial Japanese Navy, my friends and relatives aided in the preparation of my scarf of a thousand threads."

"I don't believe I've met a Kamikaze pilot before."

"Kamikaze?" Rocco asked.

Blossom laughed. "No, Chief. Reincarnation is not one of my bits. I was indeed a Kamikaze pilot in 1945. My most honorable and venerable grandfather talked me into it. The dirty bastard almost got me killed."

"I find it rather unusual that you're still here," Lyon said.

"Not really so miraculous. I joined the group in May 1945. My squadron was poised for destruction of the American fleet at the time they invaded the homeland. As we all know, that never happened, and the remaining Kamikaze pilots survived. There were a few die-hards in the squadron who wished to dive on the *Missouri* during the signing of the articles of surrender, but members of the royal family were able to dissuade them. So you see, gentlemen, my life was spared through the intervention of a man-made blossom."

"The atomic bomb," Lyon said.

"Yes. The destruction of Hiroshima and Nagasaki showed me the way. I knew then, in a brilliant flash of godly intuition, the fate of the world and my purpose in it."

"Which is?"

"The world will destroy itself, of course." As Blossom

 talked he became filled with a deep intensity and an almost beatific look. "Yes, the world will die in 1982. In a multitude of brilliant blossoms, the world will perish, and only the chosen will survive."

"Through your intervention?"

"Oh, no. I am a practical man. Through the inhabitation of deep caves in the abandoned Colorado mines. We are already arranging the purchase of our shelters. The people of the Blossom will survive and populate the earth with a true feeling of brotherhood."

"If the earth is going to destroy itself, why the great interest in acquiring material things?"

"Like money, Mr. Wentworth?"

"Exactly."

"The purchase even of abandoned mines and all the necessary accouterments for prolonged existence requires money. Just as we view the atomic wars to come as a real possibility, we are pragmatic in our fund-raising efforts. We live in complete love, and we invest as wisely as my meditation allows."

"Such as a one-fourth interest in the Darling Corporation?"

"I expect that ultimately that will be quite lucrative."

"Particularly with Giles and Esposito dead."

"God moves in mysterious ways."

"Doesn't the reduction of your investment group through murder bother you?"

"You may have noticed that we have excellent security here at the house of the Blossom. No, it doesn't bother me. My disciples will defend me—to the death if necessary."

"You knew Tom Giles?" Rocco asked.

"But of course. He was our attorney, arranged our incorporation in this state and the purchase of this property, and we were partners in the Darling Corporation."

"And Sal Esposito?"

"I never met the man. I knew the name, and that he was a co-investor in our land deal, but the papers were signed separately, and we never met."

"Where were you the night of the murders?" Rocco snapped.

"Here, at the house of the Blossom."

"Can you verify that?"

"Of course. As I recall, I was receiving two new members, brothers Early and Winston. When new members join the brotherhood, I like to spend a good deal of time with them for initial orientation. We have marathon sessions of meditation and prayer."

"For the time of both murders?"

"Yes. The same brothers."

"I'd like to talk to them," Rocco said.

Dr. Blossom sighed. "The media and so many in authority doubt my veracity. It's a pity, you know. My message of survival should not go unnoticed."

"I'd like the message from brothers Early and Winston," Rocco said.

"Of course." Blossom pressed a recessed button on the side of his chair, and a robed figure appeared instantly in the doorway. Blossom rose and extended his arms outward as the beatific look returned. "Oh, dear brother, would you bring brothers Early and Winston to me?"

"Yes, Reverend."

"I would prefer to speak with them alone," Rocco said.

"I would have imagined that would be your procedure. I shall leave you."

Brothers Winston and Early, their shaved heads glistening, sat stiffly upright on the edge of the settee. They reminded Lyon of first-day students sitting expectantly before him. He wondered what ingredients of naïveté, idealism and alienation had brought them here. Salvation is a heady brew; spice it with brotherhood and it becomes an intoxicant. A far cry from his own mild immersion in the clear waters of New England Unitarianism—a religion he recalled someone's saying was a little bit about love, a little bit about God, and mostly about Boston.

"Were you two together the day and evening of the thirtieth?" Rocco asked.

The two disciples exchanged bewildered glances. "Why do you want to know?" one asked.

"Which one are you?"

"Brother Winston."

"I'll ask the questions, Winston."

"We are new disciples. It was our orientation period."

"Together?"

"The two of us—and of course the Reverend."

"And the evening of the sixth?"

"The same."

"If you're so concerned about us," Winston said petulantly, "ask Dr. Blossom. We were with him. Are you trying to bust us?"

"You were with the doctor on both occasions?"

"Ask him."

"I have," Rocco said.

The Reverend Dr. Blossom took the earphones off and gently laid them on the table.

"I think those kids would lie to hell and back for their leader," Rocco said from the driver's seat.

"The Mouse in the Monastery," Lyon replied. "This mouse has to proselytize the larger rats in order to save the books; the learning of the ages must be preserved."

"Oh, Christ!" Rocco said and almost ran into the gates before they were opened.

Bea sat dejectedly in the breakfast nook as Robin perched on the kitchen counter, her arms akimbo. The young girl's eyes flashed as they swept past Lyon leaning against the wall.

"Thanks a lot, you guys. You didn't tell me I was going to be the only girl on that hulk."

"I thought you'd enjoy that part," Bea said. "ALL ALONE WITH MEN."

"You need a new battery in your hearing aid," Robin said.

Lyon thought he heard a deep internal rumble from his wife as she stiffened.

"Can you imagine what it's like being seasick and having forty guys chase you over the rigging so they can show you how to tie square knots in the anchor locker?"

"Where'd you jump ship?" Lyon asked.

"Nantucket. And I hitched back."

"What have you and Rocco been up to?" Bea asked.

"We'll bring you up to date," Lyon said as they filed into the study.

"I hope somebody hid the chalk," Kim said.

Rocco and Lyon described their interviews with Damon and Dr. Blossom. Each man amended the other's statements until the nuances and feel of the day's conversations were apparent to everyone.

"YOU KNOW, IT'S A PRETTY DUMB THING FOR GARY MIDDLETON TO HAVE LEFT THE MURDER WEAPON AROUND SO IT COULD BE FOUND."

"Without it, the State Police wouldn't have enough to convict."

"Then they aren't taking the investigation any further?" Kim asked.

"No," Rocco replied. "From this point on, all their efforts are directed toward building a case for the prosecution against Middleton and Karen Giles: developing witnesses to their affair, subpoenas for financial records, the ballistics evidence . . ."

"Couldn't Damon Snow have left the party the night Esposito was killed, and then sneaked back? We might not have noticed."

"I know he was here all that night," Lyon said.

"Then it's got to be Dr. Blossom and his crew of nuts," Bea said.

"And he has two witnesses who are willing to swear they were with him at the time of both killings," Rocco said.

"What about the Manson case?" Robin asked.

"How's that?"

"They never actually proved that Manson killed anyone personally. Only that he directed his clan to do the killings. Couldn't these so-called disciples of Dr. Blossom have been in the same position?"

"Without an informant, there's no way to get near that type of conspiracy," Rocco said.

"We have to infiltrate the Blossom people," Lyon said.

Bea laughed. "I can see the newspapers now: Secretary of the state resigns, prominent children's writer and local police chief throw over all to join Blossom people."

"You're not getting me into any white robes," Kim said.

"I've seen them on the streets with their salad bowls," Robin said. "The average age of those kids is nineteen."

All eyes turned to the young girl sitting Indian-fashion on the floor.

"Did you say nineteen, dear?" Bea asked.

"Now, wait a minute!" Robin said, jumping to her feet. "That ship was bad enough, but you aren't exiling me with a bunch of religious freaks."

"You can wear your bikini under the robes," Bea said with a smile.

11

"Can't this hick town find a better place to have a meeting than this dump?" Captain Norbert picked up a shot glass and glared at the streaks along the sides.

Sarge Renfrow threw a damp bar rag and yelled, "Four cops in here don't exactly help business, you know!"

Rocco waved. "Another round, Sarge."

Norbert covered his glass with a palm. "We've got to get going. What else do you want to know?"

"How about putting surveillance on Dr. Blossom?"

"You're the one who's always yelling about jurisdictional rights. *You* do it."

"In the first place, Norbie, I don't have the manpower. And secondly, my men aren't trained for that sort of work."

"What do you have on Blossom?"

"Motive."

"And an alibi for the time of both killings."

"Yes, but that could be phony."

Captain Norbert tapped Rocco's badge. "You got as many years in this business as I do. You ought to know by this time that we can't stake out everyone with a motive. We'd need the Russian army for manpower."

"I think you have an obligation, Norb."

"Bullshit! The prosecutor thinks he has a case, the grand jury will return an indictment, and my job is help them hang Giles and Middleton."

"Wait a minute."

They were off again, Lyon thought, as he twirled his glass and looked out the dusty barroom window. In a field across the street, two boys were flying a kite. It was a large one, shaped in the form of a black falcon, and the day's quick breeze puffed it higher and higher. It bobbed and circled toward the radio station's transmission tower, and if the boys let out more string, it was doomed to fatal entanglement in the steel girders.

The kite bobbed between two girders, weaved out once, and then was hopelessly caught above the ground. The larger of the boys tugged on the string until it snapped. His shoulders slumped as they both stared disconsolately at their entangled toy.

A vague thought began to nibble at the rim of Lyon's consciousness. He reached for it, but it disappeared, leaving shadowy trails of a wispy but unformed conclusion. He would start at the beginning— He turned to see the two senior police officials shaking fingers at each other, while the two corporals fought to look impassive and choke back laughter. "I want to see the Esposito house again," Lyon said.

Norbert turned to glare at him. "Will you keep out of my hair, Wentworth?"

"If he wants to see it, let him," Rocco said. "Sometimes he comes up with things."

"Wouldn't if I could. The special task force on

organized crime has the house sealed. Forget it."

"Where's the houseboy? What's his name?"

"Koyota," Rocco said. "You want his home address?"

"Uh huh," Lyon said.

Lyon braked the Datsun behind two mopeds at the red light on the edge of the Murphysville green. He impatiently clenched and unclenched his fingers on the steering wheel while awaiting the turn of the light, and then he saw them at the corner. They stood by the main entrance of the Connecticut National Bank. While her partner extended his bowl toward passersby in a hostile and belligerent manner, Robin smiled, and the long white robe failed to hide the full dimensions of her figure. As Lyon watched, two men hesitated, stopped, and fished for coins.

A horn behind him honked and he threw the car into gear. Dr. Blossom had found his most effective beggar. He realized that he missed her, and he thumped the steering wheel to dispel the unwelcome visions. He must think only of the Japanese houseman and what he might learn from him.

Koyota, wearing a silk gown and a neatly tied ascot, opened the door and peered myopically at Lyon. He blinked in recognition. "Mr. Wentworth."

"I wonder if I might talk with you a moment."

He bowed. "I am at your service, but, most regrettably, at this time I have certain acquaintances present."

"It's most important."

"I am at your service. Perhaps in"—he looked at a large chronometer strapped to his wrist—"an hour."

"Hey, Snake, hurry up," the deep feminine voice echoed from the rear of the apartment. Koyota threw up his hands in resignation and opened the door for Lyon.

The apartment was a large one-room efficiency with a Pullman kitchen. Two of the biggest women Lyon had ever seen reposed in the huge bed in the corner.

"We having a party, Snake?"

Houseman Koyota sank into a deep circular divan and crooked a finger over his shoulder. "Drink. Your preference, Mr. Wentworth?"

"A sherry if you have it."

Koyota clicked his fingers, and immediately the women, dressed in panties and bras, slipped into peignoirs and began to mix drinks. They were amazons, and Lyon found it difficult to keep his eyes off the six-foot blondes. He began to speculate about the small man in the ascot and the large women, but abandoned these thoughts for the business at hand.

"What did you wish, Mr. Wentworth? My employment perhaps? As you know, I am available for the right person under the right circumstances."

"Martini, Snake?" the second woman asked shyly.

"Dry, and don't bruise the gin."

"No, not employment. I have some questions concerning the death of your former employer."

"Most regrettable. A man of discerning taste. It was a pleasure to work for him. I informed the authorities of all that I know, which was very little." He stuck his hand in the air, and the martini was immediately placed in the palm.

"You spent the day working on the house, prepared dinner at six, and then left for the evening."

"To get ashes hauled."

"Ah, yes," Lyon said and could not help glancing at the women, now perched on bar stools. "And you found the body. Tell me about that."

"Why? I have been over this before."

"There might be something that would help. Please, once again."

"I arrived at the house a little before eight, entered, and began to prepare breakfast. When I attempted to serve Mr. E., I found his room undisturbed. A few minutes later, after going through the house, I found his body. In the pool. I called the police. That's all."

"Yes," Lyon mused. "I saw the body when we arrived. Fully dressed, with shoes on. You also said that the night before, you prepared a meal of *gohan, suimono, sashimi* and *chawan mushi.*"

"*Tsukemono* and *tempura* also."

"Does it take long to prepare such a meal?"

"Minutes if the custard has been made earlier, as mine was."

There's nothing there, Lyon said to himself; no clue of any sort. A routine he went through as on any other day. He cleaned the house and pool, served dinner, and returned the next day to find his employer dead. The errant thought solidified: "Mr. Koyota, you told us that you spent several hours working on the pool."

"Yes. Mr. Esposito was most particular about the pool. He allowed no chemicals of any sort, and he insisted that it be thoroughly cleaned once a week."

"How do you clean a pool?"

"Really quite simply, Mr. Wentworth. You drain it, climb in with a brush, and scrub."

"But Esposito drowned in the pool that night."

"After I finished my cleaning, I closed the drains and let it fill."

"Which would be about what time?"

"Just before I began to prepare dinner."

Lyon grabbed Koyota's arm. "Do you have a key to the house?"

"An extra one in my bureau."

"Then come on, Snake, let's get over there!"

The unhappy Japanese remembered to have Lyon remove his shoes as they entered the foyer. He turned to stare wistfully at Lyon's car parked at the curb. "Last time I left those two alone, they got into the vodka and solicited the doorman."

"I'll hurry," Lyon said and walked quickly toward the pool room, leaving Koyota struggling to replace the police seal on the door.

The pool seemed to echo as he stood on the tiled edge and looked down into the empty basin. A dim, clouded light came through the glazed ceiling. He sat and let his feet dangle over the edge.

Minutes later he heard the slither of the panel to his rear. "Are you finished, Mr. Wentworth?"

"No. Would you fill the pool, please?" Lyon pushed off the tile and fell lightly to the floor of the deep portion of the pool. "Can you remember exactly where you first saw the body?"

"About halfway toward the steps."

"Please start the water."

As Koyota left the room, Lyon walked the length of the pool and back. By the time he had reached the deeper part, water had begun to rush through a two-inch pipe recessed into the wall in the eight-foot-deep section. He watched the water a moment as it began to trickle around his bare feet.

"Anything else, Mr. Wentworth?"

"Yes. Adjust the water to full pressure."

The Japanese shook his head and again disappeared. Shortly, the water flow increased. Lyon watched it a moment and then retreated halfway toward the steps. He lay on his back on the dry tiles.

"You'll get wet, Mr. Wentworth, and we should go."

"Uh huh," Lyon replied and looked upward toward the indistinct day beyond the skylight.

"Mr. Wentworth . . ."

"Yes? Why don't you take my car and go back to your friends? Please return in exactly five hours to pick me up." He reached into his pocket, fished for the car keys, and tossed them to the waiting man.

"Five hours?"

"To the minute, please."

As he heard the front door close, he crossed his arms under his head and tried to make himself comfortable on the hard surface. The sound of rushing water was not unpleasant. He closed his eyes. *The Parrot at the Pool*—yes. It might make a story. A sylvan glen, deep in the forest, with a clear pool of cold spring water. The animals, of all sorts, would follow the shaded paths to the pool, where the parrot reigned. He would have to think about that.

"By God, I think the silly bastard is trying to drown himself!" Captain Norbert's voice reverberated through the tiled room as Lyon's eyes slowly opened. He felt chilled, and as he turned to face the offending voice his nose and mouth filled with water. He gasped, choked, and sat up.

"Get out of there, Lyon," Rocco said from the pool's edge.

"I was worried, Mr. Wentworth," Koyota said from behind Captain Norbert. "And so when I was ready to come back, I called Chief Herbert."

"How long have I been in here?"

Koyota looked at his oversize wristwatch. "Four hours and fifty minutes."

"Get the hell out of there, Wentworth, or do I have to come in and drag you out? This building is police-sealed."

"In a few more minutes." Lyon turned to face the deep end of the pool. It was now completely filled. Sitting in the water, he noticed that it had risen to lap around his thighs. "What happens when the pool is filled?"

"The water never cuts off. When it reaches the drains, part of it is automatically let out and recycled so that there's a constant interchange of water."

"Are you coming out of there?"

"I want to double-check my estimates."

"You have broken a seal. You can get a bust for that, Wentworth."

"O.K."

"Damn it all, Rocco, he's your friend. Get the crazy out of the water."

"You had better come out, Lyon."

"Few more minutes."

"Bust the bastard," Norbert said to the ever-present corporals.

From the corner of his eye Lyon saw the two police corporals jump off the side of the pool, grimace as the water seeped through their pants, and advance toward him. One pulled a blackjack from his back pocket, the other a pair of handcuffs.

"Wait a God damn minute!" Rocco yelled and jumped into the pool. His huge bulk caused a large gush of water to splatter Captain Norbert. "You lay a hand on him and you'll deal with me!"

"Are you interfering with my orders?" the enraged Norbert bellowed.

"That's right." Rocco reached down, grabbed Lyon by the shirt front, and jerked him erect.

"Cut it out, Rocco. I'm not finished."

"Yes, you are." He threw Lyon's weight over his shoulders, splashed to the end of the pool and let Lyon fall on the tiles. "Now, what in hell were you doing?"

"What time did Esposito die?"

"You know damn well when. The medical examiner is positive that he was killed at midnight . . . give or take a few minutes either way."

"No, not killed. That's when he died."

"I don't understand your semantics."

"Esposito had dinner served exactly at six. He had probably finished at seven. He was called outside, where he was coshed."

"Coshed?" Norbert asked.

"The victim was rendered unconscious," Rocco translated.

"He was placed unconscious in the shallow end of the pool," Lyon continued. "And was drowned some five hours later."

"How in hell do you know that?"

"I just timed it."

Rocco looked at Lyon silently for a moment and then extended his hand and helped him to his feet. "Damon Snow."

"It's possible."

"He could have been knocked out and thrown into the pool at midnight," Norbert said. "It could have happened either way."

"I know," Lyon said. "But you have to admit it is interesting."

At the Thursday 10:00 A.M. tour of the toy factory, Lyon felt out of place. He wasn't quite sure whether the unsettling feeling arose because the young tour guide reminded him of Robin, or because of the twenty-three chubby children who surrounded him as the tour formed. He had noticed the school bus when he parked the car. A sign along its body announced: "Camp Tonowanta—Slim down with a summer of fun."

As the kids gathered around him at the entrance to the factory, he noticed that several of them, behind the counselor's back, were surreptitiously passing candy bars back and forth.

The tour guide, who had "Wendy" emblazoned across her red sports jacket, smiled and held up a hand.

The group fell silent except for the crunching of a nut bar, which caused the counselor to turn and glare.

"The first department we will visit is where the famous Wobbly dolls are made. Has everyone heard of the Wobblies?"

There were murmurs of assent as Wendy looked directly at Lyon. "For you older folks, the Wobblies are famous monsters who are characters in a children's book series."

"Sounds vaguely familiar," Lyon replied, and wondered when he would ever be able to get to the next Wobbly story.

"All right, keep together now."

The tour for Lyon was a kaleidoscope of impressions: long cutting tables where moving knives shaped dozens of patterns at once, high-speed sewing machines connecting the various parts of the Wobblies, and stuffing machines which pounded fill material into the monsters at the rate of a dozen a minute. He stood before a one-way mirror watching the testing room where small children played with new toys and games.

Fingers tapped his elbow. "We're moving to the cafeteria for refreshments, sir."

"We haven't been in the east wing yet."

"That's the research department, where new lines are developed, but I'm afraid it's off-limits for us."

"Secrets?"

"Oh, yes. New lines must be kept from the competition until the toys are on the market."

"That's interesting. What are they developing?"

"I really don't know." She handed out illustrated brochures and began to shoo the group toward the cafeteria.

"A rest room?"

"Second door to the left."

As he walked toward the rest rooms, he saw the guide

disappear into the cafeteria with her entourage. He hurried down the hall toward the east wing until he came to a heavy metal door with a red and white RESTRICTED AREA sign. He tried the handle, found that it turned, and stepped inside.

He found himself in a large, well-lighted workroom. "Hold it right there!" The security guard reached for the walkie-talkie snapped to his belt.

Within three minutes, Damon Snow was ushering Lyon from the east wing. "If you wanted a tour of the factory, I would have gladly given you one myself."

"I'm interested in the east wing."

"No can do, Lyon. You can't imagine how cutthroat toy competition is. I wouldn't let my own mother in there."

"You've always said I was part of the Cedarcrest toy family."

"So's my mother."

12

Kimberly Ward sat on the ground at the edge of the stand of pines and stared morosely down from the promontory toward the river. Distant night sounds provided an appropriate background for her unease. Nutmeg Hill loomed darkly behind her. She shook her head in an attempt to break the gloom. A hot bath, milk, and a dull book to fall asleep with might do it. Or she could take the car out on country roads and drive the limit until dawn streaked the sky and exhaustion enabled her to tumble into bed.

At first she had thought her state of mind was without cause, an occasional happening that overtook her without warning. It could have been caused by the day's earlier incident at her office, when an employee had accused her of reverse bigotry—favoring blacks over whites. She shook her head violently and thought of her daughter away at school, immersed in African studies, dressed in Swahili robes, who now accused her mother of being an Oreo. "I've got to be either one or the other," she said aloud.

She looked up at the dim figure moving toward her across the lawn and smiled. "That you, Lyon? Come talk to me. I'm in a real funk." She stood and started toward him.

The blow startled her more than it hurt, but its force was sufficient to knock her sprawling backward against a pine trunk.

"Hey!" The running figure passed and was lost in the pines, and she yelled: "God damn it! You . . ." Her voice was lost in the night, and she crawled to her feet to look toward the darkened trees.

She hurried toward the main house. The back-door handle refused to budge. Locked? The Wentworths never locked the back door. She tried desperately to turn the handle back and forth, than began to knock on the windowpane. "Lyon! Bea!" They were both heavy sleepers. She ran around the house to the front door and found it also locked. It was impossible to enter the house through the combination storm-window/screens without destroying or removing the fixtures. She stood below the master-bedroom window and yelled.

Smoke curled through the living room window. Tongues of flame sputtered near the couch in the center of the room, and toward the front, fire leaped at the draperies. She knew that a large stone at the corner of the patio parapet was loose, and she threw it through the window. She put her legs over the sill and fell onto the floor. The choking smoke made her cough as she struggled for the stairs.

She fumbled with the door of the master bedroom, stumbled inside and lurched toward the bed to shake Bea's shoulder.

"Not again, Lyon," the sleepy woman mumbled.

"Bea! Lyon! For God's sake, the place is on fire!"

They both awoke and sat up. Kim snapped on the overhead light and slammed the door shut as smoke billowed up the stairwell and into the room. Lyon coughed and reached for the bedstand telephone to dial 911. He looked at the receiver incredulously and dialed again. "The line's out!"

"Someone came from the house, hit me, and ran into the woods."

Lyon nodded as he leaped from the bed into a pair of trousers. "We'd better go out the window." He heaved a straight-backed chair against the window and screen, carrying glass and frame away from the house. He lowered Kim and Bea by their wrists as far as he could, then released them and let them fall to the ground. He sat on the sill a moment, trying to see the ground in the darkness below, and then pushed off. As he hit the ground, he bent his knees and fell to the side in order to absorb the impact.

"Everyone all right?"

"I'll phone from the cottage," Kim said and took off at a full run toward her small house a hundred yards distant.

"I'm going to see if I can do anything with the fire extinguisher."

It surprised him that the back door was locked. He elbowed a lower pane from the frame, reached through, and turned the handle. Putting a handkerchief against his face, he went into the kitchen and by memory located the extinguisher in its mountings next to the stove.

The fire seemed to have originated in the living room. He sprayed swatches of foam in front of him as he fought his way toward the flames licking their way up the draperies.

"My phone's out, too!" Kim yelled from behind him.

"Keep it from the ceiling beams or the whole place

 will go," he said as he handed her the fire extinguisher and ran from the house. Although most of the instruments and equipment from the balloon gondola had been vandalized when he landed on the beach at Lantern City, the CB radio in the pickup was still intact.

He opened the truck and switched on Channel 9, the emergency frequency. Lyon had heard that Radio Emergency Associated Citizen Teams monitored the emergency channel on a twenty-four-hour basis. "This is an emergency! Can any REACT team hear me? I repeat, this is an emergency!"

When Lyon switched to receive, a voice answered immediately, "Middleberg REACT. State your problem."

Lyon quickly gave the location of Nutmeg Hill and asked that the Murphysville Fire Department be called.

They stood on the edge of the yard lighted by the powerful searchlights on the fire trucks. The fire had been brought under control in less than an hour; two trucks had already left, and now the rubber-coated men were searching to make sure every vestige of the fire had been extinguished.

"They didn't have to chop the front door in," Bea said softly. She stood forlornly by Lyon's side. Two large tears welled from her eyes and ran down her cheeks. She brushed them away with the back of her hand.

Lyon thought of the hundreds of hours they had worked on the house. He could see Bea, on her knees, refinishing a difficult floor by hand, or painting and scraping the widow's walk . . . and now half their home was destroyed.

Rocco Herbert flicked soot from his uniform as he stepped through the torn door. He stopped in front of Bea and put a gentle hand on her shoulder. "I'm sorry."

Bea blinked away another tear. "YOU COVER THE FIRES, TOO?"

“Only when the origins are suspicious.”

“The phone lines were cut, doors were locked that shouldn’t have been, and Kim was hit by someone running from the house.”

“And we found these,” Rocco said as he displayed a handful of rags. “For some reason this bunch didn’t go up.”

Lyon took the rags and sniffed them. “Gasoline. Pretty obvious, isn’t it?”

“Clear case of arson. We’ll dust for prints, but I can’t put much hope in that. What about you, Kim? Can you identify the man who ran past you?”

“I couldn’t even swear it was a man. A person wearing dark clothes. That’s all.”

Bea felt the rags. “Unbleached muslin. Odd material to use in setting a fire.”

“Unless you happen to have an awful lot of it,” Lyon said.

“I think the water did more damage than the fire,” Lyon said as they trudged through the shambles of the living room. They were throwing the irreparable pieces out on the front lawn for later trash pickup, and were trying to restore some semblance of order. The phone company had arrived early to repair the lines, and a crew of carpenters was already at work replacing window frames and sections of wall.

As Lyon and Bea carried the ruined divan out to the pile of trash, they saw two figures coming up the drive. Bea’s fingers tightened on Lyon’s arm. “I THINK YOU’VE GOT ABOUT EIGHT YARDS OF UNBLEACHED MUSLIN COMING UP THE ROAD.”

Lyon shaded his eyes. The girl was obviously a tousled and very tired Robin. He recognized the man as Winston, one of the disciples he and Rocco had interviewed in Blossom’s office. Robin and Winston stopped to stare at the house. The early-morning wind whipped their robes backward in a trailing stream.

"What happened?" Robin asked as Bea felt the hem of her robe.

"I'd swear that it's the same material."

"I'll call Rocco to have him run a match with the lab."

"WHAT ARE YOU TWO DOING HERE?"

Winston posed as he directed his answer to Robin. "We are apostates. I would tear these unholy robes from my body, except that . . ."

"I think he's bare-assed underneath," Robin said.

"I'll find you something to wear," Lyon said as he took the young man's arm.

At one time in the dimness of his past, Sarge had been a mess cook. He made very passable fried eggs and bacon, although the toast was scorched when he took a moment off to tipple. They had left the house, which was now swarming with workmen, to drop off the robes at Rocco's office. Realizing that it was close to ten and that they were famished, Bea and Lyon had driven to Sarge's Bar and Grill.

"They evidently do some sort of investigation on new members," Robin said through a mouthful of egg.

"I could have told you that if you'd asked," Winston added pompously.

She smiled at him. "Anyway, after I'd been there a few days, the great Reverend calls me into the inquisition. Winston and his cronies were there, standing behind Blossom like they were going to put me in the Iron Maiden or something. Blossom had found out that I'd been staying at your place, and he knew I was a ringer. To make a long story short, they kicked me out."

"And Winston?"

Robin brushed her companion's cheek. "Winston escorted me to the gate and kept right on going."

"When was all this?"

"Yesterday afternoon."

"Why did you arrive at the house only this morning?"

"We couldn't seem to pick up a ride, not with those ridiculous robes and all, so we had to hoof it. We found some kids with a camper at the state park, and we crashed with them last night."

"Then Dr. Blossom must have thought you returned to the house last night. He would have expected you to be sleeping here."

"I guess," Robin said, and started on her fourth egg.

Lyon looked at Robin's companion. Dressed in slacks and a sport shirt, he looked even younger. At all times, his attention was directed toward Robin. He stared at her with the look of a starving man, as if trying to consume every word and action. "Why did you leave, Winston?"

"Because of Robin."

No more had to be said on that score. Winston had discovered a new religion that would be more powerful than his last. "You were one of the disciples who were with Dr. Blossom at the time of the murders."

"No, sir. We said we were, but we weren't."

"You lied?"

"Dr. Blossom told us that there was a plot by his enemies to get him and destroy the order. To save everyone, we had to protect each other at all costs."

"And now you're telling the truth?"

"I swear it. Dr. Blossom was not with me those times."

"The preliminary lab reports indicate that the cloth we found in your house and the cloth in the robes are very similar."

"But not to the exclusion of all other cloth?"

Rocco turned the car off Route 92 at its junction with Plank Road. The mansion occupied by the Blossom people lay four miles up the twisting road. He shrugged in response to Lyon's question.

Lyon turned to look out the window. The rock-strewn fields, with their long lines of hand-built walls, stretched interminably along the tree-shrouded road. "We might prove it if we could lay our hands on more of the cloth."

"How's that? The state lab is pretty damn efficient, and if they say it's not conclusive . . ."

"The robes we gave them as samples may not be from the same run."

"What are you talking about?"

"Robin tells me that the Blossom people make their own robes, that they're running a veritable cottage industry at the mansion. Now, the robes she and Winston were wearing might have been from a different run."

"Run?"

"They probably buy their bolts of cloth wholesale. Each bolt, each run, will have its own minutely distinctive characteristics. If we could get our hands on other robes or on some unused muslin that came from the same lot . . ."

"It could be conclusive."

"Exactly."

As they turned out of a curve they found themselves facing an oncoming vehicle straddling the crown of the road. It was obvious that there would be insufficient space for the cars to pass. With a guttural "God damn!" Rocco wrenched the wheel and spun the car into the loose rock wall along the shoulder. The police car's right wheels jounced along the low wall as the car tipped dangerously and Rocco fought for control.

As the other vehicle sped past, the car tilted more precariously and slid into a skid that spun them around to face in the opposite direction.

Rocco slumped over the wheel briefly, and then,

swearing, tried to start the stalled car. The starter motor whirred ineffectively for a moment and then caught. The cruiser jerked forward.

"You're going the wrong way to get to the mansion," Lyon said.

"Mansion, hell! I'm catching that crazy son of a bitch who almost killed us!"

He had the car at seventy before they reached the junction and turned north on the highway. In the distance, they could see the car they had almost collided with. Rocco accelerated, and from morbid curiosity Lyon leaned over to watch the steady climb of the speedometer needle.

"You're doing over a hundred!"

"Freddy was right; those dual carbs help a lot."

"We're going to have a dual funeral."

"That bastard will pay for this!" He flipped on the siren and flashing roof lights.

"Why don't you radio ahead for a roadblock?" Lyon yelled over the din of the siren and the strange clanks from the car's dented body.

"Screw the roadblocks. This guy's mine!" They were gaining on the other car. "It's a damn Rolls," Rocco yelled and pressed the accelerator to the floor. "I've got him!" he said gleefully. As the distance narrowed between the two cars, the Rolls reduced its speed until Rocco pulled abreast of it and signaled for the driver to pull over.

"Do you see who's driving that car?"

"Blossom."

Rocco walked toward the Rolls, taking care to keep directly behind the driver. His right hand gripped the butt of his pistol as he yanked the door open. He pulled Blossom from the car and forced his hands onto the car roof as he patted him down.

"Leave the Reverend alone!" Blossom's companion

 had rushed Rocco and was pummeling his shoulder with her fists.

"He's only doing his job, Lorelei," Blossom said. "Remember our precepts of love."

The girl stepped back and then bowed her head. "Leave him alone," she said in a more subdued voice.

"He won't be hurt," Lyon said.

The girl wrenched her arm away from his touch. Her face seemed to elongate as her lips parted. Lyon wouldn't have been surprised if she had actually snarled at them.

"Into the cruiser, you two," Rocco said.

As the town library was closed for the day, Rocco opted to use those facilities. Dr. Blossom sat at the reference table with his hands folded before him. The robed girl at his side still glared with unabashed hostility. Lyon sat at a table in a far corner as Rocco placed the arrest report in front of Blossom.

Dr. Blossom methodically took glasses from his pocket, balanced them on the edge of his nose, and read the report slowly. "That's quite a list, Chief. My attorney will call it harassment."

Rocco signed the report. "Speeding, reckless driving, leaving the scene, driving on the wrong side, improper license. There must be more if I can think of them." He put the report aside. "There is one more item I'm thinking of charging you with."

Blossom put his glasses away. "Oh?"

"Murder."

"You seem to be very much alive."

"Tom Giles."

"You know very well that my whereabouts are accounted for during the periods in question."

"Your alibi doesn't stand up. The Winston boy will sign an affidavit stating that he was not with you. You made him alibi for you."

“Apostate!” the girl screamed.

Blossom patted her hands. “It’s all right, my dear. The faithful will survive. I have many enemies, both individual and institutional, that wish to destroy me and the movement.”

“The only destruction I’m interested in is that of Tom Giles and Esposito.”

“Since I began the movement, I have been accused of everything from mail fraud to kidnapping, Chief Herbert. But never of murder.”

Rocco unwound from his easy slouch on the chair and walked methodically toward Blossom. He placed his hands flat on the edge of the table and leaned forward with his face inches from the minister’s. “You were aware that the land deal would be more profitable with fewer survivors. You killed Giles and then Esposito. After Winston left the mansion, you tried to burn down the Wentworth house and kill them all.”

“Preposterous!”

“We found gasoline-soaked rags that had been used to start the fire. The same material as that!” He pointed an accusing finger at the girl’s robe. “And you have no alibi left, Blossom!”

The girl stood. Her long fingers gripped the edge of the chair as she shook with intensity. “He was with me. Both times. With me. He didn’t want anyone to know about it. We . . . we were making love.”

Blossom splayed his fingers in a gesture of resignation. “Continence is not a tenet of our movement. For diplomatic reasons it is best that my foibles not be advertised.”

“And if we break her down, there’re others?”

“Probably. Now, I think I’d like to see my lawyer.”

“He’s dead,” Lyon said quietly.

“There are others, Mr. Wentworth. There are always others.”

13

They were alone in the library. Rocco had taken Dr. Blossom down the hall to the telephone and had left Lyon with the disciple staring belligerently at him across the room. Her piercing look never left his face, as if she blamed her leader's recent troubles completely on him.

He spread his arms. "Isn't love one of your precepts?"

She snorted and turned away to pick up a newspaper suspended from a wooden rod in a rack. As she opened the daily to hide her face, Lyon saw the banner headline: KAREN GILES ARRAIGNED.

He stretched his legs onto an adjoining chair and tilted back. The discovery of the handgun in Gary Middleton's home would be the final piece of circumstantial evidence needed to convict Karen and her lover. And yet, their present residency in jail precluded their participation in the arson of Nutmeg Hill. The Blossom people had great quantities of unbleached muslin, and the movement's leader was an experienced pilot, while Damon Snow was not.

He idly glanced along the line of reference books stretched across the table and began to flip through the pages of *Prominent Eastern Industrialists.*

Damon Snow did not warrant a long listing:

"Snow, Damon Lamont: Toy manufacturer, b. Ridgewood, N.J., May 8, 1932; s. Wilburn Thornton Snow and Ida (Hunt) Snow; student . . ."

Lyon skimmed the remainder of the listing and then went back: ". . . Served with U.S. Army 1951–53, Captain, Art. Recipient of American Defense Medal, two Korean Battle Stars, Bronze Star, Distinguished Flying Cross and Purple Heart."

Rocco slammed the door and gestured to the disciple to leave. "His lawyer's here arranging for his release on his own recognizance, and all I've got on the Oriental bastard is a handful of traffic violations."

"What about a search warrant to find the cloth match?"

Rocco's glower was replaced by a sly smile. "Maybe, just maybe."

Bea's dungarees had ripped along a seam, her shirt was smudged, and soot streaked her cheek. She stood on the front stoop as Lyon kissed her.

"How is it?"

"OUTSIDE OF A MEDIUM-RARE LIVING ROOM AND EIGHTEEN MILLION GALLONS OF WATER, WE'RE IN GOOD SHAPE."

"Except for the loss of your hearing aid."

"IN MY BACK POCKET."

He snaked the small device from her pocket, adjusted the level, and placed it in her ear. "Robin giving you a hand?"

"Robin and Winston have been in the barn all morning."

"Separate stalls, I hope."

“ALL RIGHT, WENTWORTH. How come you always sneak out every time the house burns up?”

“This is the first time . . .”

She laughed. “How about coffee? The kitchen’s in good shape.”

The kitchen wasn’t actually in good shape. Smoke smeared the walls and sooty water streaked the floors, but it was relatively undamaged. Bea hastily boiled water and spooned instant coffee into mugs. “By the way,” she said, “the office called, and your Dr. Blossom is having his religious charter challenged by the IRS.”

“That’s interesting.”

“I thought you might think so. I called the station and left the same information for Rocco.”

Lyon stirred the steaming coffee and stared into its black depths. “How do you get the Distinguished Flying Cross when you’re in the artillery?”

“You get shot out of a cannon.”

“Very funny.”

“Don’t they use helicopters a lot? I would suppose those men must be entitled to flying decorations under certain conditions.”

“During the Korean War, helicopters were used mostly for rescue work and evacuation of wounded.”

“What does that have to do with the price of anything?”

“Damon Snow was in the army, and yet he’s the recipient of a flying medal.”

“During World War Two, what is now the Air Force was the Army Air Corps.”

“Not in 1950.”

They turned simultaneously as the barn door slammed. Winston strode across the yard, followed by Robin, who grabbed his arm and spun him around. They engaged in a very animated argument.

“Doesn’t he have a home?” Lyon asked.

"Some suburb of New York. Sooner or later I suppose his parents will come after him."

"They're having a hell of a row. You don't suppose he molested her, do you?"

"YOU'VE GOT TO BE KIDDING! Nobody says that any more. I think she's trying to molest him."

"That's unfair."

"I fear, dear Lyon, that your solicitousness smacks of the prurient."

"Come on. The thought never entered my mind." And he wished it hadn't.

He parked on a side road and crossed the fields to a small rise, bracketed by a clump of trees, across from the Cedarcrest Toy Company. He found a shaded spot where he could lie prone to steady the binoculars and watch the factory's afternoon shift change.

He swept the area around the factory with the glasses. Snow had chosen the site well. The factory was located off an excellent highway, just across the small Morgan River. A well-kept lawn led toward the landscaped buildings. To the rear of the property was a long meadow that would provide room for future expansion. He swung the binoculars back to the rear field and examined it more closely. He estimated that it was a thousand yards in length and a hundred wide, with meadow grass that had been mowed recently. After it was dark he would have a closer look at the pasture.

The traffic jam at the parking lot had begun. The departing cars lined up at the covered bridge over the river and were directed out onto the highway, while a shorter incoming line of cars waited at the highway to cross the bridge toward the parking lot.

He had a mental profile of the man he wanted. One likely prospect drove a dented VW into the lot, but Lyon lost interest when the occupant reached across the seat for his suit coat and briefcase.

A '70 Chevy with flaking paint captured Lyon's interest. The car's engine revved impatiently until the security guard signaled it through the covered bridge toward the lot. It jerked forward with a puff of dirty exhaust. He followed the car's progress with the glasses and noticed that it squeezed into a slot near the employees' entrance and chugged to a halt.

Lyon examined the driver carefully as he slammed the car door and slouched toward the building. He seemed to be in his early fifties and wore heavy work shoes and splotched denim pants. A black lunch box was tucked under one arm, and a frown curled his face. Beaded perspiration on the man's forehead and a red-veined nose made Lyon decide that this was his prospect.

At ten minutes to twelve he parked the Datsun next to the peeling Chevrolet. He glanced around the lot and then quickly crossed to the Chevy to raise the hood and pull out the main distributor wire. He put the wire in the Datsun's glove compartment and sat back to wait.

The man with the reddening nose looked even more dour as he crossed the lot. As he shoved himself into the seat, Lyon deliberately overchoked the Datsun until the smell of gasoline was noticeable. Both men tried in vain to start their cars.

"Who's the son of a bitch?" the red-nosed man said as he threw open the hood.

Lyon leaned out his window with an ingenuous smile. "Pardon?"

"Some bastard took my distributor wire. You see anyone?"

"My car won't start, either."

"You've flooded it," the man snapped and slammed the hood. "It's that rotten little runt Joey. I'll kill the bastard!"

Lyon inwardly cringed at the anger seething within

 the man. He knew that a missing wire would annoy most people, but the hate that spewed from the other man enveloped them both. He tried the ignition again and heard the starter motor whine and catch.

"Can I give you a lift?"

The man turned suspiciously. "How do you know you're going where I'm going?"

"Doesn't make any difference to me. I'm from the outside auditors, and I'm staying in a motel. I always drive around before I turn in."

The man glared a moment and then yanked the car door open. "Why the fuck not?"

His name was Bill, and he drank boilermakers. They hunched over the scarred booth in the neighborhood bar, sipping whiskey and tossing down beer. "Joey hates my ass," he said.

"You're in maintenance, aren't you?"

"How'd you know?"

"Must've seen you around today."

"Right. Custodial maintenance. That means shit jobs. What the hell, for five bucks an hour I'm not complaining."

"Not as much as those guys in the closed section make."

"You mean where they make the new stuff?"

"They really pour the money in there."

"How do you know about that?" Bill asked with a squint.

"I'm an auditor. We have to go over the books once a year. I know how much they spend for that sort of thing. But I don't know what they're making."

For the first time, Bill almost smiled. "They got great stuff in there."

"Like what?"

"All this good mechanical stuff. Not like those dolls they make in the factory."

"You mean they're designing wind-up toys?"

"No, good stuff—rockets and airplanes, all that kind of stuff."

"Rockets?"

"Right. Damnedest thing. Couple weeks ago they were setting them off in the field behind the plant. Little bastards, maybe three feet high. They look like the real thing. When they take off, man, they really go."

"How will you get to work tomorrow?"

"Hell, Joey will take me. And when he goes inside, I'll take *his* fucking distributor cap!"

As Lyon left, Bill was still morosely drinking and looking as if he would continue to do so until the bar closed. He drove back to the toy company, parked on the same side road he had used earlier, and approached the field behind the factory by a circuitous route.

A half-moon reflected dim shafts of silver light from behind scudding clouds as he climbed fences and walked through knee-high grass until he was behind the building. He pulled a penlight from his pocket and slowly paced the width of the field with downcast eyes.

Near the center of the field he knelt beside a thin swatch of parted grass. It had been a dry month, and no rain had fallen since Tom Giles's death. The impressions in the soft loam were quite distinct as he ran his fingers over the wheel indentations. The penlight's small glare clearly outlined the tread marks.

A powerful battery lamp cast a circle of light for a dozen feet around Lyon. He stood and shaded his eyes from the beam shining directly into his face. "Who's there?"

"Communing with nature, Lyon?"

"Is that you, Damon?"

"Sit down. That's right. Right there. Sit down and clasp your hands behind your back. Go on!"

Lyon did as instructed. "I know your voice, Damon. I think you should know that Rocco is out here."

The man behind the light laughed. "Come on, Lyon, don't sound so dire."

"How did you know I was here?"

"Security spotted you when you crossed the field. I was working late, and when they recognized you, they called me." He turned the light away from Lyon's face. "Put your hands down. Now, what are you doing out here in the middle of the night?"

"Tom Giles's plane landed here."

"I'll put up a monument."

"During your military service you were . . ."

"In the artillery."

"As an observer pilot. A spotter flying fixed-wing light aircraft."

"If you're interested in my military career, Lyon, I'll send you a copy of my service record."

"You did fly?"

"Of course I did."

"I wouldn't be surprised if we matched the tire tracks in this field to the tires on Giles's plane."

"That doesn't prove anything. Now, what are you getting at?"

"You were involved in the land deal with Giles and Esposito."

"So was Blossom."

"You stood to benefit by their deaths. You fly, and Giles's plane landed here."

"And I was with you when Giles's plane went down."

"Not with me. I was in the balloon."

"I could hardly have left, killed Giles, taken his plane, flown it into the sound, and been back at the house in time to help you search for him."

"No, you couldn't have."

"You know something, Lyon? Your breath smells like you've been drinking. Go home and sober up."

14

She stood on the porch with her feet apart. Her voice crossed the T and hit him broadside as he stepped from the car. "ALL RIGHT, WENTWORTH! WHERE HAVE YOU BEEN FOR TWO DAYS?"

He fingered his ear as a gesture for her to turn up the hearing aid.

"IT *IS* TURNED UP! I'M MAD! TWO DAYS, WENTWORTH!"

"There was a lot of checking to do. Then the trip to New York for the materials, and then the practice."

"Where in New York?"

"F. A. O. Schwartz."

Her voice dropped to a near-whisper. "How much?"

"About three hundred."

"I'll double that to six."

"And eighty-five cents."

They walked into the house arm in arm. "You know,

 Lyon, if I hadn't known that your paramour was in our barn all this time . . ."

"Both of them, still . . . ?"

"No, he moved into the bedroom the other night."

"What bedroom?"

"The guestroom, goose! They've been arguing like two old marrieds. Now, where have you been?"

The phone rang just as Rocco's police cruiser screeched to a halt in the drive. "No, Kim, you can't quit until I'm back on Monday," he heard Bea say as he went to meet Rocco.

The police chief scowled at Lyon. "AND WHERE IN HELL HAVE YOU BEEN FOR TWO DAYS?"

"*Your* hearing, too?"

"What?"

"Never mind. Come on in."

"I haven't had any sleep in two days."

"Worrying about me?"

"Hell, no! Sitting outside Blossom's place waiting for the creep to make a wrong move. When he does, I'm going to crucify him."

"The cloth?"

"Still negative."

"I'm not surprised," Lyon said as they entered the kitchen.

"Come the revolution, Kim," Bea said, "they'll need people like you in government."

Lyon poured three mugs of coffee and tried to hand one to Bea at the phone but was waved away. "There are airplane-tire prints in the field back of Damon's factory. I've also found that he can fly. If we take plaster casts of those markings in the field, and match them against the Giles plane . . ."

"Being deputy secretary is not selling out!"

"That's easy enough to do," Rocco said.

The kitchen door slammed open. Winston stood

wild-eyed in the center of the room and pointed at Lyon. "I'm not ready to settle down to write children's books. I don't even like children! You've got to drive me to the recruiting office right away. The Marines want good men!"

"Let me lay it out for you about Damon, Rocco. First . . ."

"Today! I have to join today, Mr. Wentworth!"

Lyon turned to face the agitated young man. "Why the Marines?"

"My hair's already short."

Robin had followed him through the door. "You're love's apostate . . . an adolescent."

"I've had enough of that!"

"And I can't stand two unrequited love affairs," Robin said.

Bea looked away from the phone. "With all the time you two have spent in the barn, I would have thought you would be well requited." She turned back to the phone. "No, Kim, not relieved, requited, and I didn't mean you."

"She's bugging me to death," Winston said.

"That doesn't take much!" Robin yelled.

"EVERYONE SHUT UP!" Lyon ordered. He took the phone from Bea. "Kim, this is Lyon. We'll see you later tonight." He hung up and turned to Robin. "Call your father and make arrangements to go home. Now! Rocco and I will drop you off at the bus station, Winston. Where's your home?"

"Larchmont, but I took a vow of poverty."

"I'll advance you the money. Get in the car."

"Yes, sir."

"Rocco, we need to make a cast of the tire print in the field."

"For a moment I thought you were going to send me home, too."

As Rocco parked in the toy factory lot, Lyon looked toward the rear of the building in astonishment. A tractor had almost finished plowing the long field. Long parallel rows of earth had been freshly turned by the massive blade.

"I should have come back the next morning," Lyon said softly. "Like a fool, I wanted to put the whole thing together."

"A little late in the season to be planting," Rocco said. "Let's ask Mr. Snow about his agricultural plans."

"Winter wheat," Damon said with a bemused look and swiveled his chair. "Or is it summer wheat? I always get them mixed up."

"In Connecticut?" Rocco asked.

"Maybe some corn, then."

"There's a charge called willful destruction of evidence," Rocco said.

"What evidence?"

"Those airplane tracks in the field," Lyon said. "I saw them, and you saw them with me."

"I don't know what in hell you're talking about, and I'm getting damn mad about this whole matter. All I know, Lyon, is that you've been seeing things for the past couple of weeks. Seeing and hearing things that no one else sees or hears. I know artists are unstable, but these delusions of yours are becoming psychopathic."

"You deny there were any tracks in that field?"

"Absolutely."

"You work two shifts here, don't you?" Lyon asked.

"During the week."

"Then a worker or one of your security people would have seen and heard that plane land and take off."

"At least your delusions take logical form. We don't work any shifts on the weekend. The plant is buttoned up; we have a fine alarm system and teams of guard dogs. As I recall, the Giles plane went down on your birthday, Sunday."

"And there would have been no one here that day?"

"Except the dogs we use for those occasions."

"I'm afraid they make very poor witnesses, Lyon," Rocco said.

"Then you have a choice, Chief," Damon said. "Either Lyon is a good witness or he was seeing things."

"He's usually right."

"In that case, he knows we were all together when he saw that plane go down."

Rocco turned to Lyon. "*Two* planes, but of similar color and make."

"Not exactly," Lyon said. "But I think I can show what happened that day. Perhaps you'd both like to join me at sunrise tomorrow morning at Damon's place in Lantern City?"

"Wouldn't miss it for the world," Damon said.

Lyon arrived at Lantern City Point before dawn. Working quickly, he laid out the balloon, went through the inflation process until the balloon bobbed off the ground, and moored it to the pickup's bumper. He began to arrange the other items as quickly as he could.

As red sun streaked the eastern sky, Rocco's cruiser, followed by Damon's Lincoln, turned off the main road toward the house at the far end of the point. Rocco's car pulled ahead and stopped parallel to the pickup. The police chief slammed out of the car and strode toward Lyon, now standing by the erect balloon.

"I'm playing along, Lyon. But I'd like to know what you intend to prove."

Lyon checked the level on the propane tank. "I'm going to show you how it was done."

"By Dr. Blossom?"

"I don't think so."

"Blossom could have used Damon's field to land and hide the plane. He had a motive, he was a flyer during the war, and the cloth we found in your house after the fire is similar to the disciples' robes. Finally, his alibi doesn't hold up."

"You never could match the cloth."

"He could have destroyed that bolt; he had the time."

"There may be another source for that cloth."

Damon Snow parked next to the cruiser and ambled toward them with his usual bemused look. "Morning, gentlemen. I assume the demonstration is nearly ready?"

"It is."

"I've already seen how your balloon works," Damon said as he plunked into a lawn chair.

Lyon reached into the balloon basket and gave the propane burner a flick. The long flame streamed into the envelope with a small roar that stabilized the position of the balloon. "Rocco, please get into the basket."

"You're out of your mind! I'm not going up in that thing."

"Get in. There're things I have to do on the ground."

"I don't know how to operate it."

"Do exactly as I tell you."

"Hell, I could blow over Long Island Sound and go down in the drink!"

"I'm not letting you off the mooring line. You'll go up about a hundred feet, and I'll keep the line attached to the bumper of the pickup. Come on, in the basket."

Rocco shook his head but nevertheless swung his legs into the gondola. The added weight made the basket sink toward the ground. "Now what?"

"The propane burner on the control panel was broken when I crashed on the beach, so you'll have to operate the lever over your head. Put on the asbestos glove, and when I give a swinging motion with my hand, give it a three-second burn. O.K., now!"

Rocco reached gingerly over his head and flipped the small lever. More flame shot into the envelope. "Like this?"

"Now, if I cut my hand across my throat, immediately let go of the lever. Give it five more seconds."

Rocco flicked the lever for the required interval. "Nothing's happening."

"How much do you weigh?"

"Two eighty-five."

"Give it a ten-second burn."

As the propane burn continued, the balloon began to bounce gently from the ground, and then it quickly rose. "Cut!" Lyon yelled, and the whoosh of the burner immediately ceased. The bag ascended majestically and silently in the early light. "Every thirty seconds, give it a burn of three."

"Now what?" Damon Snow asked, with an edge to his voice.

"In a minute," Lyon replied as he looked upward to watch the balloon rise to the length of the mooring line. "Look to the east, Rocco. To the east!"

When he was satisfied that the balloon was safely leveled at the end of the line, Lyon went to the cab of the truck, turned the ignition key, and began to twirl several dials of a radio set held on his lap. "Watch to the east, Rocco," he said under his breath, and hoped the trial runs had been sufficient to enable him to operate everything properly.

Rocco Herbert's hands clutched the guy line running to the envelope ring. His knuckles turned white as he braced his feet against the three-quarter-inch plywood that formed the floor of the basket. He heard Lyon yell for him to look to the east, and he realized that in order to accomplish this, he would have to open his eyes. He blinked as the balloon reached the end of the mooring line.

The year before, perched on a swaying ladder over the second story of his house, he had realized that the added years had brought him vertigo. He had laughed at himself as an ex-ranger, once used to scrambling down sheer cliffs and parachuting from aircraft, now developing such an unreasonable fear of heights.

How in the hell had he been talked into taking a ride in this ridiculous vehicle?

The plane came directly from the east, and he shaded his eyes to look toward the rising sun. Intermittently he could see it clearly—a brightly painted craft. It waggled its wings and then changed course to head out over the sound.

A small plume of black smoke came from the engine cowling, and the plane nosed down in a power dive toward the water.

My God! It was going to hit! As he leaned toward the diving plane he felt the basket tip precariously under his shifting weight.

The plane dove into the water and was immediately lost from sight under the whitecaps of the sound.

"Get me down from here! I saw it! I saw it!"

He saw Lyon leave the cab of the truck and look toward him. "Pull the white line. And for God's sake not the red one!"

He carefully avoided the red line as he reached gingerly toward the other rope. He gave it a hesitant tug and then looked up at the apex of the envelope to see the panel move aside. As hot air escaped into the atmosphere, the balloon settled gently to the ground.

"So, what did you see?" Damon asked.

The balloon bobbed on the ground as Rocco dropped

over the side. "I saw an airplane that looked like Giles's fly out of the sun and then dive into the water." He turned to Lyon. "How did you arrange it?"

Lyon gestured toward the rear of the truck. "We can do it again, if you'd like."

Rocco swept back the tarpaulin from the truck bed to reveal another exact replica of the Giles plane—with a three-foot wingspan. "It's a God damn toy."

"The radio control's in the cab."

"We've begun to experiment with them at the factory," Damon said. "But I would imagine that Lyon already knows that."

Rocco held the radio-controlled plane in one hand. "Damn it! I saw an airplane up there!"

"You saw what you expected to see."

"Cut the riddles."

"What an object appears to be and where it is seen depend on each other. You and I, Rocco, saw a plane in the air over the water, with no reference point of known size. We perceived an aircraft of familiar size. Let me ask you how far away you thought the plane was when it went down."

"A couple of thousand yards."

"Closer to a couple of hundred feet."

"That's impossible!"

"Elementary laws of the relationship between object, image and visual experience," Damon said didactically. "If the object is of giant size, it will appear nearer; if it's a miniature, it will seem farther away."

"An optical illusion?"

"In a manner of speaking," Lyon said. "And it worked. On the morning of my birthday, Bea gave me the new gondola. It was a surprise to no one except me. Everyone knew that I couldn't resist an early-morning flight."

"It is the best time to launch, isn't it?" Damon asked.

"When I saw a uniquely painted plane come out of the sun, I assumed it was Tom Giles, and I kept that assumption."

"The engine was on fire; I saw the smoke."

"So did I. It's easy enough to rig. Two pellets placed under the engine cowling that melt after sufficient heat application."

"Then Tom Giles was murdered that night?"

"And the body was taken to the real plane, parked in back of Damon's toy company."

"Flown into the water, and the killer swam ashore."

"An inflatable raft, actually," Damon said. Rocco and Lyon turned toward the tall, thin man holding the automatic. He quickly screwed a silencer onto the end of the barrel.

"And I was your alibi," Lyon said. "You knew that I'd swear to the time the plane went down."

"As you were to be my alibi for the Esposito killing, but you saw through that one rather quickly."

"You were the only one who could have put it together. You knew we'd be at your house that day, and knew of Bea's gift."

"Give me the gun, Damon." Rocco's voice was steady, almost gentle, as he walked slowly toward the man with the pistol.

"Stop right there."

"The gun, Damon."

The weapon thumped, and Rocco fell with one leg bent to the side. He raised himself to his knees and began to crawl forward. "Drop it."

The weapon thumped again. Rocco's other leg twitched, and he fell face forward into the sand. Damon walked over to the fallen police officer and slipped the magnum from its holster.

Rocco's hand curled around Damon's ankle. As Rocco jerked the leg, tripping Damon back into the sand, Lyon rushed forward. Damon twisted to his feet and into a crouch, with the gun leveled at Lyon's midsection.

"Not another step, Wentworth!" He walked carefully around Rocco, taking care to stay away from the big man's hands, and brought the butt of the pistol down on the prone chief's head. As Rocco's face slumped into the sand, Damon unsnapped the handcuffs from the holster belt and cuffed Rocco's hands behind him. "Get the other pair out of the cruiser's glove compartment! Go on!"

Lyon entered the passenger side of the cruiser and clicked open the glove compartment. The extra handcuffs were on top of a pile of traffic summons forms. He glanced up at the ceiling, where the shotgun was bracketed. He tried to remember whether Rocco had told him the weapon was loaded or empty. He supposed the chamber would be empty, so he would have to pump a shell in.

"Hurry up!"

He glanced through the windshield to see Damon standing by the unconscious Rocco. Without further thought Lyon reached up and wrenched the shotgun from its mountings, pumped a shell into the chamber, and pointed the gun over the car door toward Damon.

Damon laid the muzzle of the automatic against Rocco's forehead. "You fire—and he gets it in the head!"

"I can't miss with a shotgun!"

"Neither can I."

Lyon knew the shotgun blast would kill Damon before he could fire more than once. Even if the automatic was able to snap a second shot in his direction, it would probably miss—although the first, fired directly into Rocco's head, could not miss. He let the shotgun clatter against the car's fender, raised his hands, with the handcuffs dangling from his fingers, and walked toward Damon.

"I don't like the way he's breathing."

"It doesn't really make much difference. Put him in the balloon."

"What?"

Damon waved the pistol at him. "You heard me. Dump him into the basket!"

Lyon dragged Rocco toward the balloon basket and, as gently as he could, lowered the inert form over the edge, onto the floor.

"Turn around," Damon ordered. "Hands behind your back."

As Lyon obeyed, he felt the grip of the handcuffs over his wrists. "What are you going to do?"

"Into the basket."

"There isn't room, with him on the floor."

He felt the pressure of the automatic's silencer against the small of his back. "You know, it doesn't really matter whether I shoot you."

Lyon awkwardly put one leg over the side of the basket, teetered a moment, then shoved upward with the remaining foot and fell into the basket, on top of Rocco. Trying to find space on the flooring where his feet would not dig into the unconscious man's vulnerable body, he struggled to stand.

"You can't do this, Damon."

"Wind's right."

Lyon looked toward the pole at the front of the house, where an American flag rippled in the stiff breeze. It pointed directly toward the water, which meant that there was a strong offshore breeze. His fears were confirmed when Damon stood on the edge of the basket. Reaching as far into the balloon envelope as he could, Damon severed the release- and ripping-panel lines. He used one of the severed ends to tie the propane lever down in the ON position. With the butt of his pistol he knocked the propane valve off the tank in the basket.

The balloon began to lift from the ground as the

propane burned directly over Lyon's head. It would be too high for him to reach with his hands cuffed behind his back.

"What would you guess, Lyon?" Damon yelled up at him. "Maybe twenty or so miles out over the water before it comes down?" Damon gave him a mock salute and cut the mooring line.

As Lyon looked down at the rapidly retreating ground, Damon seemed already to have dismissed them from thought. He was busily loading the airplane and radio device into the motorboat. It was obvious that they would be dumped into the sound.

He wished he had told Bea everything. The rush of events had given them little time together, and he had never brought her up to date on his discoveries. There was only the forlorn hope that at some later time she would go over the invoices and papers concerning his recent purchases, and perhaps piece together his theory . . . that is, if she didn't automatically destroy all his personal effects upon his death.

He braced himself against the side of the basket and watched with fascination. He had never made an ascent under these conditions and at this speed, but he could imagine the parabolic curve of the balloon as it gained altitude and, caught by the wind, swung out over the water.

Rocco stirred and moaned on the floor of the basket. Lyon looked down at him and saw blood seeping from both leg wounds. Rocco moaned again as his eyes opened. His head bobbed back and forth as he looked at the side of the basket and strained against the handcuffs.

"My God! Where are we?"

"In the balloon."

"Oh, Jesus! What's happening?"

"If the propane held out, which it won't, we'd be making the first transatlantic balloon crossing."

15

Bea knew something was wrong as soon as she opened the door. Damon Snow stood before her, his body bent forward in a tired slump, and a slackness in his narrow features.

"What is it?" she asked in a weak voice.

"I don't know how those things are supposed to work, but I was worried and thought I should see you."

"What do you mean?"

"Rocco and Lyon launched the balloon at Lantern City. They seemed to be in a hurry, as if they were checking on something."

Bea wanted to grab his shirt front and shout in his face. "I don't understand. Rocco has always sworn he'd never go up."

"There was a strong offshore breeze that blew them out over the sound, and that's the last I saw of them."

"How long ago?"

Damon looked at his watch. "Almost two hours ago."

"My God! What time did you call the Coast Guard?"

He looked puzzled. "The Coast Guard? I never thought of it. I began to worry after an hour, when they didn't come back."

"Why did you drive all the way out here when you could have called?"

"At first I thought they were headed for Long Island and would call you when they arrived. Then, when I saw the drift . . ."

"Which way was the wind blowing when you left?"

"The same as when they went up, about ten knots, from the southwest."

Bea ran for the study. Her hands trembled as she dialed the Coast Guard. The problem cascaded out in short, choppy sentences: ". . . That's right, over two hours. The tank would be empty now. . . . Wind from the southwest . . . what's the recent weather report? . . . Same wind as the last two hours. . . . Thank you. Yes, I'll call the Civil Air Patrol."

Others to call. She couldn't remember the numbers. Where was the phone book? Bea put her hands to her face for a moment until her mind cleared, and then she reached for the phone again to dial information. "This is an emergency. Please give me the numbers of the Civil Air Patrol, the Connecticut National Guard, the FAA team at Bradley Airport, and Westover Air Force Base. Please hurry!"

As she attempted to give the pertinent information in a quick, rational manner, she saw Damon in Lyon's chair, observing her. "Is there anything I can do?" he asked when she was finished with the last call.

"There's nothing more to be done."

"I'll drive you to my house in Lantern City."

"They'll be calling back here. I'd rather wait."

"What will happen to the balloon?"

"That depends on a lot of things: their altitude, how

well he conserved fuel, any air currents they might have picked up. When the propane runs out, the hot air will cool and they'll come down in the water."

"It's pretty calm out there today. An inflatable raft will save them until they're picked up."

"There isn't any raft or life jacket."

"Oh."

"I'm going to have a drink. Will you have something?"

"A scotch and water, please." He followed her into the kitchen. "I feel responsible for this. I should have stopped them."

"It's not your fault. Lyon is one of the most experienced balloonists in New England. He knew the risks."

"Why was he so insistent on going up?"

Bea took an ice tray from the freezer and stood poised by the kitchen sink. "It had something to do with the murders. Lyon had been away for almost two days checking and assembling things. He told Rocco some of it when I was on the phone yesterday. They went off, and when he came back he fell into bed mumbling that he'd tell me the whole thing in the morning. He was gone when I awoke this morning. We never did have a chance to talk about it."

"Then you don't know what he had in mind?"

She slowly dropped ice cubes into two glasses. "As I said, he mumbled something; it sounded like, 'nothing as it seems, through the looking glass. It's all in the toys.' It didn't make much sense, and he was very tired."

"No, it doesn't."

Bea mechanically poured scotch into the glasses and added tap water. "I know this. He had the answer to the Giles murder."

"Are you sure there's nothing I can do?"

"No, thanks," she replied absently and handed him a drink. "He had been in New York."

"Really?"

"He had a bunch of receipts and invoices that he pulled from his pocket and stuffed into the dresser."

"Receipts for what?"

"I don't know." She felt a chill and looked across the room toward the man looking at her with the level gaze. She slowly placed her drink on the counter. "Liquor doesn't seem to help. I think maybe I'll take a tranquilizer. Will you excuse me?"

"Of course."

"I'll be right back."

As Bea disappeared up the stairwell, Damon Snow took the automatic from his pocket and began to screw the silencer to the barrel.

Rocco had managed to sit up, with his back wedged against the side of the basket. "How are your legs?" Lyon asked.

"Could be a lot worse. He got me in the thigh and calf, but the bleeding's slowed, so he must have missed the arteries. Right now, I've got the feeling that my wounds are the least of our worries. What's going to happen?"

Lyon looked out over the edge of the basket. To the left and behind were the Race, Fisher's Island, and the distant shore of Connecticut. They had passed Montauk Point, on the right. Open sea lay ahead. "We'll go down when the propane runs out."

"Into the water?"

"I'm afraid so." They were still on the rising edge of the parabolic curve that was taking them higher into the atmosphere and farther out over the water. Lyon knew that the altitude record for a hot-air balloon was 86,000 feet, but that had been in an enclosed gondola with life-support systems. He didn't inform Rocco that once they reached 18,000 feet they would begin to feel the effects of oxygen deprivation and would start to die of hypoxia.

In the distance was the low outline of Block Island, their last landfall.

He looked up into the envelope to see the panel lines flapping uselessly. The cut lines were too deep within the bag for his handcuffed hands to possibly reach, even if he did manage to balance on the rim of the basket. Their trajectory still carried them toward Block Island. If the wind remained constant, without diverting puffs, they would pass over the northerly spit of land at the island's apex.

His mind sought frantically for the temperature and descent formulas so carefully learned years ago in ground school and almost as quickly forgotten. He slid down in the basket with his feet next to Rocco's. Lyon could figure the temperature inside the envelope, and he knew that the seventy-five degree ground temperature had fallen three degrees for every thousand feet of altitude . . . he must convert those Fahrenheit temperatures to Kelvin and try to calculate the air pressure and its effect on the balloon circumference.

"For Christ's sake, Lyon, don't conk out on me now!"

Lyon shook his head vehemently and closed his eyes. There were so many variables, and it was almost impossible to work out the equations accurately in his head. He lay back against the wicker and cleared his mind of everything but the applicable data.

Lyon blinked his eyes open to face a frightened Rocco. He struggled to his feet to look at the small finger of land still in the balloon's path. "We can make it to Block Island if we can manipulate the burner."

"How?"

"Can you get into a squatting position?"

"I don't know."

"If you can, and if I throw my legs over your shoulders while you stand . . . I may be able to reach the rope around the burner lever."

"It's worth a try." With a grimace of pain, Rocco drew

 his leg up and shoved himself forward until he was kneeling on the swaying basket floor. Lyon swung his legs over Rocco's shoulders and tucked his feet under.

"Can you stand?"

"I've got to." Rocco placed one foot flat on the floor and involuntarily let out a groan of pain. His body wavered for a moment, and then the other leg went forward until he was bent forward in deep-knee-bend position, with Lyon swaying on his shoulders. "Here we go!"

Their bodies leaned from one side to the other on the unstable platform as Rocco slowly rose. Lyon pulled his cuffed hands up as far as he could. His fingers searched for the rope tying the lever.

"Oh, Jesus!" Rocco said as his right leg splayed to the side and both men crashed down against the side of the basket. "I can't do it, Lyon. My legs won't hold up."

Time was running out. The propane had to be adjusted immediately in order for the balloon to have a gradual, constant descent toward the spit of land that was less than a quarter of a mile in width. A miss of a hundred yards in either direction would mean drowning. Lyon wondered briefly how long he could tread water if he was able to escape the confines of the collapsing envelope, but he knew that Rocco, with his injured legs, would be completely helpless.

Rocco turned his head toward the propane tank. "Why don't you just turn the thing off from here?"

"Damon knocked off the valve."

"Pull out the connecting hose so the damn thing won't feed fuel."

Lyon shook his head. "There's too much pressure in the tank. If we pull out the hose, the propane will blow up toward the burner and we'll turn into a fireball."

"Then don't let it all out."

Lyon nodded his head. "It might work." He hunched

across the basket toward the tank and sat on its edge, with his hands behind him around the connecting hose. His fingers fumbled at the holding brackets at the base of the tank and gradually worked them loose. The hose broke free from the tank, and a short gasp of propane rushed past Lyon's neck before he jammed a finger in the aperture.

Over their heads, a burst of flame broke around the burner. "Is the pilot light out?" Lyon yelled.

"I don't think so."

As the air in the bag cooled, they began to drop. When the rate of descent increased, Lyon fumbled for the loose end of the connecting hose and awkwardly worked it over the nipple. The burner burst into a long streak of flame. He left the hose attached for a count of five and then jerked it away from the tank and covered the opening.

The balloon began a stepped approach toward the island, until at 1,200 feet the propane gave out. They began to drift rapidly and noiselessly downward.

As they passed over the leading edge of the island at a hundred feet, a small boy walking the water's edge looked up and waved.

"How are we doing?" Rocco asked from the floor of the basket.

"We're not going to make it," Lyon replied. "We're still at 80 feet, and we're now approaching the far end of the island. I think we'll touch down on the other side—in the water."

"In the water, you said?"

"Yes."

"I could sum this up in one word."

Lyon looked toward the horizon to see only open sea as they passed over the island. The basket skimmed the water. "If we can stay afloat for a few minutes, someone may come out with a boat."

"Do the best you can. I'll float like a rock," Rocco said as he struggled to his feet.

Lyon looked at his friend with compassion as the forward edge of the basket skipped along the waves and settled into the water. Their combined weight pushed the gondola under. The bag slowly began to fall sideways as the last of the heated air cooled and seeped from the aperture of the envelope.

They stood in the sunken gondola under the warm morning sun as the basket settled to the bottom and water lapped at their waists. "Tide's out," Lyon said in a faraway voice.

Rocco threw back his head and began to laugh. The sound spewed out in a choking gurgle that took on body and rolled out over the water. Lyon joined in, and waves of mirth convulsed them both.

Bea took the receipts from the drawer where Lyon had wadded them and spread them along the top of the bureau. He had purchased a hodgepodge of items: electronic parts, toy airplanes, chemicals. What did they add up to?

"Find anything?" Snow asked from the doorway.

She turned. "Damon! You startled me."

"Can you make anything out of what he left?"

"It doesn't make any sense." Things nibbled at the corner of her mind, and she hastily stuffed the receipts into her slacks as Damon watched her with searching eyes. "Come on, let's finish that drink."

He followed her downstairs. "Perhaps I should look them over."

She waved to him nonchalantly. "I don't think I want to fool with it now." In the kitchen she freshened their untouched drinks. "Do you remember the name of that girl who had identification in the Giles plane? The one who didn't exist?"

"Carol Dodgson."

"Yes, that's what I thought it was." She was immediately sorry she had asked. Damon sat on a kitchen stool and watched her speculatively, as if waiting for her to proceed. What had Lyon said as he tossed in his sleep? "Through the looking glass." Carol Dodgson . . . Carol through the looking glass. Charles Dodgson, Lewis Carroll's real name. Lyon had also told her about the first interview in Damon's office, with dozens of Alice dolls posed around the room. And Damon knew how to fly. The receipts had something to do with airplanes, radios, perhaps something that was radio-controlled. If anything happened to Lyon, the list could be duplicated. She could go back to the stores and purchase the same items, and that would reveal what Lyon had discovered on his abortive last flight.

"A penny for your thoughts."

"I'm just worried sick about Rocco and Lyon."

"I'm sure there'll be word soon. This waiting is nerve-wracking. Let me see those papers; perhaps I can make something out of them."

"I really don't care to go into that now."

Damon walked to her and reached toward her pocket. "I said, let me see them."

"Damon, please!"

He extracted the papers from her pocket and retreated across the room. Bea felt cold, very cold, and hugged her body with both arms.

The Coast Guard helicopter made a deep bank over Lantern City Point. Lyon braced himself against the vibrating airframe and looked out the window toward Damon Snow's summerhouse below.

"Can you see anything?" Rocco called from his stretcher on the floor.

"The pickup's still there, and your car, but Damon's is gone."

"We'll get the bastard. He has no way of knowing we've been picked up, and he won't be running."

"But Bea called the Coast Guard," Lyon said, his voice lost in the din of the engines. "He must be with her." He beckoned to a crewman for his headset and mike. "This is Wentworth," he said to the pilot. "It's extremely important that you take a heading over Murphysville."

"What's up?" Rocco yelled.

"I think he might be with Bea. We can tell when we fly over the house."

"Tell him to land on the Murphysville green. I can pick up some men. And under no circumstances is anyone to contact Bea."

Lyon nodded and stared numbly out the window as the helicopter followed the path of the Connecticut River toward Murphysville.

Damon glanced through the bills and invoices, wadded them into small balls and placed them in an ashtray. He set fire to their edges with a lighter.

"You don't have to burn them. I'll remember."

Damon stared at the burning papers. "I thought you might. Too bad."

"Why did you do it?"

"Money."

"Lyon figured out how it was done—something about radio-controlled airplanes. You've done something to Lyon."

"They went for a ride in his balloon."

Bea felt waves of nausea. She lunged across the kitchen toward the door and wrenched it open. Snow's arm curved around her neck and bent her backward. She kicked, and heard him grunt as her foot caught his shin. He shoved her onto the floor in the breakfast nook. She crawled to her feet and saw him in the archway, holding the automatic.

"I don't suppose it will help any to tell you that you can't get away with this?"

"I expected better of you, Beatrice."

"What will you do with me?"

"There will be a phone call shortly—from the Coast Guard, I would imagine—and afterwards you will kill yourself in a state of deep sorrow."

"I will not."

"Don't be naïve."

Robin had come through the open kitchen door and stood behind Damon with her mouth open.

"You don't imagine that I'm going to cooperate, do you?"

"You don't need to."

Robin reached across the stove to the pegboard holding a multitude of pots and pans. She quietly removed a frying pan and with both hands brought it down on top of Damon Snow's head. The automatic clattered to the floor as he fell straight forward.

"Daddy always said iron skillets were better than Teflon," Robin said as she stepped over Damon.

Lyon rode next to the driver in the first car, as Rocco tried to make himself comfortable in the back seat. They were followed by another Murphysville cruiser, a commandeered taxicab occupied by three coastguardsmen, and two State Police cars that had been hurriedly summoned off the Interstate.

"A plan of attack?" Lyon asked as he turned to Rocco.

"At the top of your drive, one car will go around the side and cover the rear. We'll go toward the living room side, and two cars will park broadside in front. We'll have the place surrounded in seconds."

"Seconds," Lyon said as the cars screeched off the highway and up the winding drive. He snapped the shotgun from its brackets over the sun visor and pumped a shell into the chamber. The cruiser swerved off the drive onto the grass and rocked to a halt.

Lyon flung himself out the door in a full run toward the living room window. He held the shotgun over his head as he calculated his approach to the bushes, and at the last moment he leaped for the window and crashed through.

He landed in a shower of glass and wood splinters and somersaulted into a crouch, with the shotgun wavering before him.

"NOT THE WINDOW, WENTWORTH!" Bea yelled as she threw herself into his arms.

"Your face is going to be a mess," Robin said as she tied the last knot in the extension cord binding Damon Snow's arms.

16

The six-foot Wobbly doll perched on the edge of the patio parapet balanced Lyon's drink between its paws. Summer night shrouded the house as a dim lantern cast faint illumination over the semicircle of lawn chairs. Lyon Wentworth, awkward in his neck brace, splinted arm, and cut face covered with small bandages, tried to smile.

Rocco lumbered out the kitchen door, supported by a cane in one hand and balancing a tray of drinks in the other. "Here they come."

"How come Rocco gets shot twice, but Lyon is the one who ends up looking like that?" Bea asked.

"Some of us go through doors rather than closed windows," Rocco replied as he passed the drinks.

"Tell Kim to join us," Lyon said.

"I did, but she's in your study writing out her resignation."

"I asked her to make it detailed," Bea said tiredly,

"and the last time I looked she was on page thirty-two and still going. With luck, the project might carry us through until the next election."

"I don't understand who tried to burn the house down," Martha Herbert said.

"Damon Snow's attempt to implicate Dr. Blossom. The arrest of Karen Giles was convenient, and he tried to assure her conviction by planting the murder weapon in Gary's house, but in order to be the final member of the tontine, he had to get rid of Blossom."

"Then he stole the unbleached muslin from the mansion?"

"No." Lyon turned painfully to pick up his drink from between the Wobbly paws. "Look at the Wobbly's face. It's made of unbleached muslin."

"All right," Bea said. "I believe you and Rocco when you tell me you saw a toy airplane that looked like a real airplane because of perspective—but why didn't we see it take off from the beach house?"

"They're really more than toys; quite sophisticated, in fact. Damon had experience with a similar drone from his hitch in the artillery. They're used, or at least used to be, for antiaircraft gunnery practice. He had the controls in the boathouse, but the plane itself was launched from Sand's Point, across the cove." Lyon decided it was the final somersault through the window that had sprained his neck.

"And you were positive it was Tom Giles's plane."

"I expected to see what I saw."

"But if Giles was still alive when the radio plane went down, Damon was taking quite a risk," Rocco said.

"Not really. He talked with Giles before killing him, and he thought he had established that Tom had been alone all that day at the lake house and that he hadn't contacted anyone. I think the reason Tom called me was to have a witness in front of Damon, but Damon didn't know that."